Tom Taylor

The Overland Route

A comedy, in three acts

Tom Taylor

The Overland Route
A comedy, in three acts

ISBN/EAN: 9783337102692

Printed in Europe, USA, Canada, Australia, Japan

Cover: Foto ©Andreas Hilbeck / pixelio.de

More available books at **www.hansebooks.com**

THE OVERLAND ROUTE.

A Comedy,

IN THREE ACTS.

BY TOM TAYLOR,

Author of "An Unequal Match," "Contested Election," "Plot and Passion," "Hearts and Hands," "Still Waters Run Deep," etc., etc.

AS FIRST PERFORMED AT THE THEATRE ROYAL, HAYMARKET, LONDON, APRIL, 1860.

TO WHICH ARE ADDED,

A DESCRIPTION OF THE COSTUMES—CAST OF THE CHARACTERS—ENTRANCES AND EXITS—RELATIVE POSITIONS OF THE PERFORMERS ON THE STAGE, AND THE WHOLE OF THE STAGE BUSINESS.

———◆———

NEW YORK:
ROBERT M. DE WITT, PUBLISHER,
No. 33 Rose Street.

CAST OF CHARACTERS.

Theatre Royal, Haymarket,
London, April, 1860.

Mr. Colepepper (Commissioner of Badgerypore District)..........Mr. CLIPPENDALE.
Major McTurk (in charge of In-(valids)....................Mr. ROGERS.
Sir Solomon Fraser, K. C. B. (ex-resident at several Native Courts).....................Mr. COMPTON.
Mr. Lovibond (a Singapore Mer-chant).....................Mr. BUCKSTONE.
Tom Dexter (an Adventurer).......Mr. CHARLES MATHEWS.
Captain Smart (of the P. and O. Steamer, Simoon).............Mr. BRAID.
Hardisty (First Officer of the Si-moon)...................Mr. WORRELL.
Captain Clavering (of the Com-mander-in-Chief's Staff).......Mr. E. VILLIERS.
Tottle (Head Steward of the Si-moon)...................Mr. CULLENFORD.
Moleskin (a Detective).........Mr. CLARK.
Limpet (Sir Solomon' Man)......Mr. COE.
Mrs. Sebright..............Mrs. CHARLES MATHEWS.
Mrs. Lovibond............Miss WILKINS.
Miss Colepepper.........Miss TERNAN.
Mrs. Grimwood (her Maid)....Miss WEEKES.
Mrs. Rabbits,.............Mrs. GRIFFITHS.

Ayahs, Stewards, Lascars, Passengers, etc.

SCENERY, Etc.

ACT I.—Scene: The Saloon of the "Simoon" under the poop deck. A long cabin, lighted from a large skylight in the coiling. The doors of the births are uniform in appearance, the upper panels closed with green Venetians. The saloon is handsomely decorated. Through the two doorways at the end, a view of the deck of the steamer. A table in the centre with seats round it.

ACT II.—Scene: The poop deck of the "Simoon," towards evening; a tropical

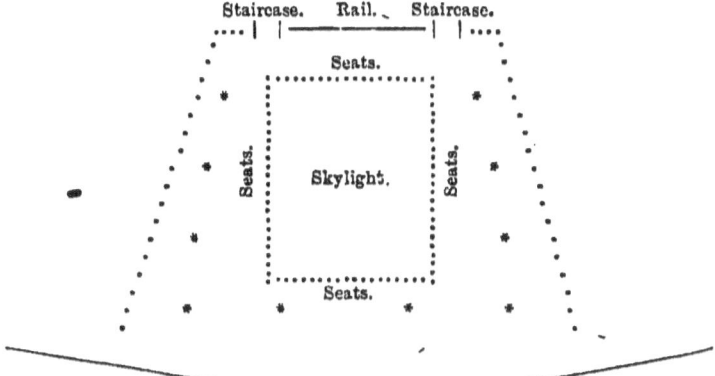

sunset sky; an awning spread; cabin skylight combings seen above the deck, with seats round them; seats at the gangways; companion seen beyond the skylight. At the back, the rail bounding the poop deck, with openings for the staircases leading to the waist of the vessel. Lounging chairs disposed about.

ACT III.—Scene: A coral reef coming down to the edge of the sea, which is seen

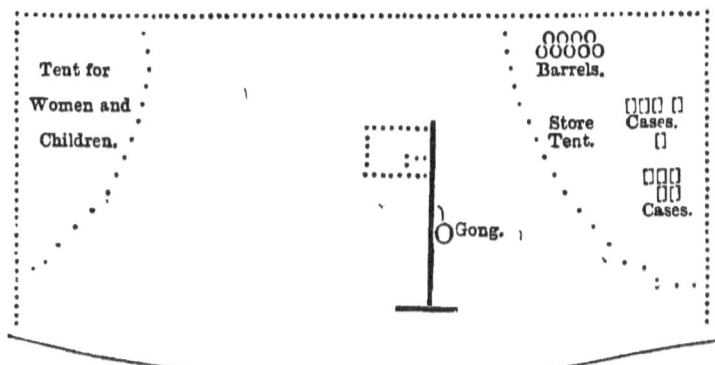

in flat. Rough tents rigged out of spars and sails, R. and L. That to the R. is the tent occupied by the women and children; it occupies three entrances. That to the L., which projects so as to intercept part of the sea view, is the store tent. Barrels, cases, wine and beer bottles, and preserved meat cases are partially visible, piled about and under it; a gong hung on a spar near it, and a flag hoisted on a flagstaff.

COSTUMES.

MR. COLEPEPPER.—Suit of nankeen, with white jean vest; low-cut shoes.

MAJOR McTURK.—Fatigue uniform coat, white pants and vest, the latter with gilt buttons.

SIR SOLOMON FRASER, K. C. B.—Rich India dressing gown, white vest and pants; low-cut shoes.

MR. LOVIBOND.—White cotton night cap, and white flannel dressing gown. *Second dress:* Check pants and vest, linen ; light tweed coat.

TOM DEXTER.—Plain tweed travelling suit, light in material, dark in color. *Second dress:* Surgeon's uniform of P. and O. S. S. Company.

CAPTAIN SMART.—Uniform of P. and O. S. S. Company.

HARDISTY.—Uniform of first officer of the P. and O. S. S. Company.

CAPTAIN CLAVERING.—Undress uniform of captain in Hon. E. I. Co.'s service.

TOTTLE.—Steward's uniform of P. and O. S. S. Co.

MOLESKIN.—Suit of dark blue nankeen.

LIMPET.—Suit of white linen. *Second dress:* Guernsey shirt, and red plush breeches.

MRS. SEBRIGHT.—Fashionable dress of handsome India sprigged muslin.

NOTE.—In *Act III.* the characters have different hats, caps, shoes, from those worn in *Acts I.* and *II.* ; and every article should have a careless and hap-hazard appearance. [*For Properties and Stage Directions see last page.*]

SYNOPSIS OF THE PLAY.

As the title of this play indicates, the action of the piece brings out in strong relief the incidents of a voyage from India in an Oriental steamship. *Acts I.* and *II.* occur on board the steamer ; *Act III.* on a desolate coral reef. The piece has many capital and strongly defined characters. It is not possible to do anything like justice to the great merits of this play, either as regards plot or characters, by a brief sketch—but the following outline may give some general idea of the piece. Among the heterogeneous ingredients thrown together in the saloon of the steamship Simoon, are MR. COLEPEPPER (with an only daughter, and she was passing fair), a rich commissioner ; SIR SOLOMON, a high India official ; MAJOR MC-TURK ; a CAPTAIN CLAVERING, a staff-officer ; an attractive married lady, MRS. SEBRIGHT ; a dashing married lady, MRS. LOVIBOND ; several officers of the ship, and though last not least, TOM DEXTER. MR. COLEPEPPER and SIR SOLOMON are both desperately in love with MRS. SEBRIGHT, and each offer her very tempting inducements to bestow her hand upon *him.* The lady plays them as a skillful angler does a trout ; but keeps them well out in the stream. Meanwhile MCTURK is quite as busy seeking to captivate MRS. LOVIBOND, who is equally tantalizing in her behavior. MR. COLEPEPPER's daughter all this time is closely attended by CAPTAIN CLAVERING, who appears to have won her confidence, though not her affections. This is the state of affairs when one TOM DEXTER appears upon the scene. This individual (who *en passant* is a splendid character), suddenly appears amidst all this cooing and billing, upon the CAPTAIN's invitation, brought about in this manner: the ship's surgeon is stricken down with fever, but his place is more than filled by the volunteer services of TOM DEXTER, a steerage passenger, who, besides being a skillful *medico,* proves himself an able and considerate adviser and consoler. The CAPTAIN brings TOM into the cabin, inducts him into the sick doctor's place, and TOM, nothing loth, soon becomes the ruling spirit of the scene. He soon gives MRS. SEBRIGHT to understand that her flirtations may not be so innocent as she deems them ; makes MRS. LOVIBOND mind her p's and q's ; cuts the comb of CAPTAIN CLAVERING ; and brings to MISS COLEPEPPER's recollection the fact that her life was saved during the Sepoy mutiny by a gentleman not unlike TOM DEXTER. There is an under current of broad farce running through this piece. MR. LOVIBOND had bought the ticket of a man accused of a felony, and had given the name corresponding to the ticket, a detective shadows him, and a variety of droll situations grow out of this queer misunderstanding. In *Act III.*, when the whole party are thrown upon the desert reef, the lion's skin is dropped, and all the personages appear as they really are. Here TOM DEXTER comes out strong, and finally through his skillful management, explanations, followed by reconciliations, take place, and everything is lovely.

THE OVERLAND ROUTE.

ACT I.

SCENE.—*The saloon of the Simoon under the poop deck.*

As the curtain rises, TOTTLE *and two steward's mates are seen dusting table and seats.*

LIMPET (*at door of cabin, No. 3,* L.). Mr. Tottle! 'Ow often am I to horder Sir Solomon's brandy and soda?

GRIMWOOD (*at door of cabin No. 2,* R.). I've been a-calling for my young lady's tea this half hour!

TOTTLE. Aye, aye, miss.—Coming, Mr. Limpet.—Jackson, brandy and soda for No. 10. (JACKSON *is going.*)

GRIM. No, we're No. 10. It's tea we want. (JACKSON *returns*)

LIMPET. We're No. 6. [*Exit* JACKSON, *perplexed.*

TOT. Aye, aye, sir. Tea for No. 6, Smiles. (SMILES *going.*)

1ST AYAH (*from cabin No. 4,* L.). Missy wants doctor very bad, massa steward. (SMILES *pauses.*)

TOT. Aye, aye. Smiles, the doctor for No. 3, and look alive!

2ND AYAH (*from cabin No. 4,* R. *Re-enter* JACKSON *with soda and tea*). Miss Polly Rabbits and Massa Charley very sick. Missy Rabbits' compliments, and hope de doctor send dem powders.

TOT. Aye, aye. The doctor, No. 4, Jackson, directly.
[*Exit* JACKSON.

HARDISTY (*putting in his head at entrance,* R. C.). Steward, bear a hand on deck here.

TOT. Aye, aye, sir. Bless my heart! Here's work for one head and the usual allowance of arms and legs.

LIMP.	⎫ *all putting their* ⎧	Brandy and soda!
GRIM.	⎬ *heads out of* ⎨	Tea!
1ST AYAH.	⎪ *their cabins at* ⎬	De doctor for missy!
2ND AYAH.	⎭ *once.* ⎩	De powders for de babies!

HARD. (*putting in his head again*). Hilloa! Saloon there!

TOT. (*hastily gives* LIMPET *the cup of tea and* GRIMWOOD *the brandy and soda-water bottle*). Aye, aye, sir! (*rushes out,* R. C.)

LIMP. ⎫ Tea! I ordered soda and brandy.

GRIM. ⎬ Man—this ain't tea!

LIMP. (*coming forward with tea*). Such attendance! Here's your tea, Mrs. Grimwood, if I might trouble you for our soda and brandy.

GRIM. Really, Mr. Limpet, it's disgraceful. I do 'ope your master will write to the *Times* when we get 'ome.

LIMP. That you may rely on, Mrs. Grimwood; if he don't make a representation to the guv'ment. Sir Solomon ain't used to this sort of thing.

GRIM. Nor us, neither, I can assure you, Mr. Limpet. What with Khitmagars, Chuprassees, and Punkahwallahs, we'd more servants up the country in Badgerypore, than we knew what to do with.

LIMP. Just like us. But, for all that, I shan't be sorry to be back in dear old Hengland, if I've to do for Sir Solomon all by myself for the rest of my born days.

GRIM. Nor me neither, Mr. Limpet. But, bless me, the tea's a-getting cold.

LIMP. And the soda-water's a-getting hot.

GRIM. Good morning, Mr. Limpet.   [*Exit into cabin No. 2,* R.

LIMP. Good morning, Mrs. Grimwood.   [*Exit into cabin No. 3,* L.

Enter, from R. D. C. *in flat,* CAPT. SMART, *a telescope in his hand, and* HARDISTY.

SMART. Well, Hardisty, as we're clear of the straits, I shall turn in for the rest of the watch ; tell the second officer to look alive, and get the new passengers shaken down.

HARD. What, with the sick and sorry, there's work for three doctors among 'em, let alone Kingston at his best ; and now he's regularly on his beam ends.

SMART. What d'ye mean ? The doctor down ! Nothing serious I hope.

HARD. I sent Tottle to inquire, sir. Here he comes.

Enter TOTTLE, R. C.

SMART. Well, Tottle ; what's the report from the doctor ?

TOT. The doctor's compliments, sir, and he's got the fever, sir ; and if the attack goes on all right, he ought to be delirious about eight bells.

SMART. Delirious ! And invalids on board, too ! Suppose it should spread.

HARD. And the ship so crowded with those Aden passengers.

SMART. By-the-bye, I've hardly overhauled the list yet, Tottle.

TOT. Here it is, sir   I was a-making out the dinner places. (*produces list.* SMART *examines it.*)

Enter MOLESKIN, *behind,* R. C.

There's one on 'em, sir—berth No. 2, there—by the name of Downy.

MOLESKIN (*aside*). Holloa ! (*listens.*)

TOT. I never see a man look so green. He said it was no use my putting him down, for his head was a-turning round so he'd be *sure* to come up t'other side of the table.

MOLE. (*coming forward*). Poor Mr. Downy !

SMART. Downy, eh ? I remember ; he's a Singapore passenger, engaged his berth from Calcutta, but came aboard at Aden.

MOLE. Ah ! I daresay he had some good reason ; which, did you say was his cabin ?

TOT. (*pointing*). No. 2, sir. Had you any business with him ?

MOLE. Oh, dear, no ! I only asked from humanity. I'm sorry he's so near the stern. He'll feel the motion very badly. (*aside*) My man, as sure as a toucher ! (*retires up and makes entries in a note-book, and strolls off,* R. C.)

SMART (*to* HARDISTY). An inquisitive customer that—always poking his nose into everybody's concerns. But about this precious business of the doctor ?

HARD. Here's the major in charge of the invalids, sir.

Enter MAJOR MCTURK, D. L. C.

MCTURK (*pompously*). Ah, Smart! Pleasant morning; a spanking breeze well on the quarter—she's doing ten knots. I've timed her. (*patronizingly to* HARDISTY) Good morning, Mr. Hardisty.

SMART. How are your invalids, major?

McT. Oh! the fellows are settling down comfortably enough. That doctor of yours is a smart hand.

SMART (*aside*). Now for it. A capital officer, major. But even doctors can't always keep their own bills o' health clean.

McT. What do you mean? Why he's hopping about the steerage like a sanitary inspector; and there he is fumigating, and airing, and Burnets-fluiding to say nothing of physicking.

SMART (*aside*). The doctor must have been taken delirious at seven bells instead of eight. I'm very glad you're satisfied, major.

McT. Why, the man's laugh is as good as a tonic.

SMART. His laugh! (*aside*) The doctor *must* be delirious! Didn't it sound rather wild?

McT. Wild! not a bit of it. Clear as a bell, and collected as a word of command. I was so pleased with the fellow that I asked for his card, a thing one's not in the habit of doing with a medico, even in the service. Here it is (*shows card*)—Dexter—" T. Dexter, M. R. C. S." I said rather a good thing, apropos of the card. " Well, Mr. Dexter," I said, " you're well named, for a more dexterous practitioner I never came across." *Dexterous*—you see. Ha, ha! Not bad was it, for an off-hand thing?

SMART. Capital! (*aside*) Who the devil can this be, I wonder?

Enter MRS. LOVIBOND *from her cabin,* 1 E. L.

McT. Ah! Mrs. Lovibond!

SMART *converses aside with* TOTTLE, *who goes off.*

In full bloom like a rose with the morning dew on it.

MRS. L. Now, Major, how *can* you? Good morning, Captain. Do you think I may venture on deck? You're sure those Lascars have done swabbing and swish-swishing about with those dreadful rope mops without handles?

SMART. Deck's as dry as a drawing-room, ma'am.

MRS. L. Then, major, may I ask for your arm?

McT. (*aside to her*). Both of 'em, my dearest lady.

MRS. L. The motion of the vessel really so throws one on some kind of support.

McT. The more it throws you on me, the better I shall like it.

MRS. L. Ah! Major!

[*Exeunt, coquettishly, leaning on the* MAJOR, L. D. F.

SMART. That's a case, Hardisty.

HARD. She's giving him a full broadside, sir, at all events.

SMART. Astonishing how these widows knock over the military. But who can this extempore Doctor be, I wonder? I sent Tottle to make him out.

Enter TOTTLE, R. C.

TOT. It's all right, sir. He's worth six of Dr. Kingston, any day; why, he makes his patients laugh on the right side o' their mouths, till they quite takes their physic with a happetite.

SMART. I never heard of a regular doctor doing *that*, eh, Hardisty ?

TOT. The women is a-blessing on him, right and left, and the babies— you'd think he'd served his time in a foundling hospital, to see the way he handles the little hinnocents.

SMART. Say Captain Smart wishes to see him aft, directly he's at liberty.

TOT. Aye. aye, sir !   [*Exit* TOTTLE, R. C.

SMART. Why, Hardisty, this is a regular god-send.

Enter 1st AYAH *from cabin No. 4,* L.

1ST AYAH. Bless me ! I wonder where dat Doctor ; Mem Sahib want him ever so bad.

Enter 2d AYAH *from cabin No. 4,* R.

2D AYAH. You just wait, please, Miss, till doctor come see my Missy babas.

1ST AYAH.	*all*	(*contemptuously*) Who your Missy baba ?
2D AYAH.	*speaking*	What your Mem Sahib, I like to know ?
3D AYAH.	*together*	Oh ! Please, Captain Sahib.

SMART. Silence ! you chattering blackbirds ! (*exeunt* AYAHS, *chattering into their respective cabins*) Just come into my cabin, Hardisty. What with Lascar crews, Madras parrots, and up country Ayahs, a fellow might as well sail Captain of Noah's Ark, as a P. and O. steamer.

[*Exeunt* HARDISTY *and* SMART, D. L. C.

Enter 3D AYAH *from cabin,* 1 R. R., *knocks at* SIR SOLOMON'S *cabin,* 3 R. L., LIMPET *looks out.*

3D AYAH. Missy Sebright's salaam to Burra Sahib Fraser, and she 'ope he gib her his arm on deck dis morning.

SIR S. (*within*). Say I shall be happy.

LIMP. Sir Solomon will be hap——

SIR S. No. On second thought, Limpet, substitute for the word happy —the word de-lighted.

LIMP. Say Sir Solomon will be de-lighted.

3D AYAH. I tell Mem Sahib.   [*Exit into cabin* 1, R. R.

Enter SIR SOLOMON *from cabin* 3, R. L. *attended by* LIMPET, *carrying his pith-cap and umbrella.*

SIR S. You, Limpet, I dare say, would not perceive any great distinction between the expressions—I shall be happy, and I shall be delighted.

LIMP. No, Sir Solomon. If I might make bold, I should think it were about six o' one and half-a-dozen of the other.

SIR S. (*with a feeble laugh*). He ! he ! he ! There are a good many men in high diplomatic positions, not a bit more discriminating than you, Limpet.

LIMP. I dare say, Sir Solomon.

SIR S. My solar topee, Limpet. (LIMPIT *gives pith-hat*) Have you consulted the thermometer this morning ?

LIMP. Eighty in the shade, Sir Solomon.

SIR S. In that case, my umbrella, Limpet. (LIMPET *gives it*) One cannot take too great precautions against exposing the brain to the sun. Limpet, the head is my weak point.

LIMP. I should think so, Sir Solomon.

SIR S. When I say "the head," understand me, Limpet, I do not mean the head intellectually considered, but the material integument of the brain. Limpet, you appreciate the distinction ?

LIMP. You mean the skull, Sir Solomon?

SIR S. Precisely. My skull is thin, Limpet—all highly organized skulls are thin,—yours is thick, Limpet; you are not highly organized.

LIMP. No, I'm only a thick-headed Limpet. [*Exit* LIMPET, 8 E. L.

Enter MR. COLEPEPPER *from his cabin*, 3D E. R.

COLE. (*comes forward*). Good morning, Sir Solomon.

SIR S. Ah! Mr. Colepepper! stirring so early ? Arn't you afraid of the morning air ?

COLE. No, sir ; nor the morning sun neither, and that's more than you can say, to judge by your precautions. (*pointing to pith-hat and umbrella.*)

SIR S. I have still a constitution to preserve, Mr. Colepepper.

COLE And I have one, sir, that doesn't require preservation. It's above proof, sir,—tried in thirty years of hard work—cold weather and hot--kutchery and jungle—hunting-field and up-country station—not dozing and dangling in lazy luxurious native courts—like some people with nothing harder to do than to nod at a nautch—or to take the air on an elephant houdah.

SIR S. Diplomatic life, too, has its fatigue, Mr. Colepepper.

COLE. I daresay. It must be hard work to keep down yawns, and to keep up appearances.

SIR S. You forget the delicate negotiations to conduct.

. COLE. As the fly on the coach wheel conducts the carriage——

SIR S. And the dispatches to be written——

COLE. From the draft of a private secretary. No, no, Sir Solomon. Don't tell an old civil servant. European diplomacy's a comedy, but Indian diplomacy's a farce very ill acted, and very well paid for. But I'm wasting my morning. (*goes to cabin*, 1 R. E., *and knocks*) Ayah, tell Mrs. Sebright Mr. Colepepper is ready to give her his arm on deck.

SIR S. (*aside*). The impertinent old interloper ! I regret, Mr. Colepepper, that Mrs. Sebright has already engaged *me* as her escort.

COLE. That was before she knew she could command my services.

SIR S. That you will allow the lady to decide. Here she comes!

Enter MRS. SEBRIGHT, 1st *cabin*, R.

MRS. SEBRIGHT. Ah! Sir Solomon! and Mr. Colepepper, too! Was ever a poor little woman so well guarded ? Two doughty squires at my beck. (MR. COLEPEPPER *takes off his cap and bows ;* SIR SOLOMON *does the same, embarrassed with his hat, stick, and umbrella*) The one armed cap-a-pie, the other cap-a-pluie.

SIR S. If Mrs Sebright will accept my escort——

COLE. My arm is always at your service.

MRS. S. Oh! bless you! I want nobody's arm—not I—I fancy I've the best sea legs of the three. It would be a positive sin to disappoint either of such *preux chevaliers*. So, Mr. Colepepper, if you would just run to my cabin and tell my Ayah to give you the novel that's on my dressing-table, (COLEPEPPER *is going*) and my shawl, Mr. Colepepper— and the footstool, please. [*Exit* COLEPEPPER, *into the cabin*.

SIR S. And now, Mrs. Sebright, that we're relieved of the old Commissioner—(*offers his arm.*)

MRS. S. Dear, dear, what a head I have! Not the gray shawl! Tell the Ayah, Sir Solomon, the white one. And my poor dear little love birds, Sir Solomon—they'll be dying for want of fresh air.

[*Exit* SIR SOLOMON, *No.* 1, R., *reluctantly.*]

Re-enter COLEPEPPER, *with novel, shawl, and footstool.*

Oh! how very good you are! (*taking the things.*)

COLE. (*aside*). She's got rid of Fraser ; now, my dear madam—(*endeavors to offer his arm.*)

Re-enter SIR SOLOMON, *with a load of shawls, cushion, and birdcage, etc.*

(*aside*) Here's that puppy back again!

MRS. S. Sir Solomon, I'm positively ashamed to see you so loaded—and Mr. Colepepper, too But you both offered me your arms, you know —and as I don't want 'em for myself--the least I can do is to use 'em for my little comforts—and when I'm snugly ensconced in a shady corner, Sir Solomon shall read to me. Won't you, dear Sir Solomon ?

SIR S. With pleasure, my dear madam, if it won't bore Mr. Colepepper. (*aside*) That ass Colepepper hates listening.

MRS. S. And Mr. Colepepper shall point out to me all the objects of interest on the coast. Won't you, dear Mr. Colepepper ?

COLE. I shall be delighted, my dear Mrs. Sebright—if it won't interrupt Sir Solomon's reading. (*aside*) That puppy Fraser hates not being listened to !

MRS. S. What a pleasant trio we shall be, to be sure! our little party will be the only one aboard the Simoon without any jealousy or heartburning, eh, Mr. Colepepper ? Quite a happy family—shan't we Sir Solomon ? With poor me to play the part of the white cat. (*going.*)

SIR S. (*aside, following her*). Colepepper for the wizened old monkey !

COLE. (*following*). And Sir Solomon for the jackdaw. (*they pass up to* R. C. D., *leading to deck. As* SIR SOLOMON *and* COLEPEPPER *try to pass out at the same door they jostle.* DEXTER *appears and attempts to enter.*)

DEXTER. Holloa ! one at a time, gentlemen ! (*the two separate and go off.* MRS. SEBRIGHT, COLEPEPPER, SIR SOLOMON, *following,* D. L. C., *in flat.*)

DEX. (*comes down*). A well-laden pair of pack asses—with Jenny Sebright, like the little bell mare, trotting on ahead. Catch *her* carrying anything ! Sir Solomon Fraser and Colepepper, too, none of the trio recognized me ! How would honest Jack Sebright like to see his "little woman," as he calls her, making a fool of these two old fogies, that ought to know better. Ah, Mary Colepepper! if Tom Dexter had a good coat on his back, and a saloon berth instead of a steerage one, he might be making a beast of burden of himself at your heels, as these old boys are at saucy Jenny Sebright's.

Enter SMART *and* HARDISTY, *from cabin,* R. E.

Oh! here's the captain ! (*touches his cap, sailor-fashion*) Well, captain, you passed the word for me ?

SMART. Oh ! You're Mr. Dexter ?

DEX. Yes. (*jumps on the table and sits.*)

SMART. Won't you take a chair ?

DEX. I prefer the table—I like to swing my legs.

SMART. I've to thank you, it seems, for taking my surgeon's duty among the steerage passengers.

DEX. Why, as they were patients without a doctor, and I was a doctor without patients. Here s my diploma—you see—licensed to drug, dose, and draw teeth *secundum artems*, and the London pharmacopœia! Don't be afraid! If anybody dies under my hand it won't be murder, but justifiable homicide—by medical misadventure.

SMART. Excuse me. But we don't often find professional gentlemen in the steerage.

DEX. Oh! I'm used to roughing it! Come, I see you're curious to know how a smart, good-looking, well-educated young fellow like me comes into this plight. (*showing his threadbare coat sleeve*) Question and answer's slow work! I'll run my story right off the reel like a log line.

SMART. Heave a-head!

DEX. I was educated for a doctor. But the practice isn't so easy to come at as the profession. As I had a fancy for the pen as well as the lancet, I took to scribbling, for want of patients—but I soon got tired of penny-a-lining, and shipped as surgeon aboard a Guinea trader. There I mastered the African fever, both as doctor and patient—got a sickener of Kroomen, palm oil, and mangrove swamps, and took a doctor's berth in one of Green's India ships. Left her at Kurrachee for a run up the country. Fell in with the Nawaub of Ramshacklegur, just as he was suffering from an awful indigestion of prawn-curry, and physicked myself into his favor. The Nawaub was a capital fellow, but he had an awkward knack of poisoning his wives when he was tired of them, and they very naturally were inclined to return the compliment. As I wouldn't agree to help the gentlemen to poison the ladies, or the ladies to poison the gentleman, of course both parties quarrelled with me, so I had to bolt into British territory to save my bacon. Then I had a shy at all sorts of things—started a hydropathic establishment at Simla, and made money—invested it in an indigo plantation in Behar, and lost it—till, somehow or other, I one day found myself installed as editor and proprietor of a paper at Badgerypore. "The Mild Hindoo," I called it—I hoped to succeed by sticking to truth and writing like a gentleman—but I soon found that wasn't the line for an Indian editor. My subscribers wanted their articles like their dinners, all capsicum and curry-powder. Just as I was thinking of cutting the concern, out broke the mutiny, and the concern cut me. My presses were smashed, my type cast into bullets; my back stock cut up for wadding—some of my articles must have had an uncommonly wide circulation in that form—and I had to run for my life? I disguised myself as a Fakir—buff and wood ashes—and doctored my way down to Calcutta, where I soon picked up enough to pay my passage home—and here I am.

SMART (*shakes hands with him*). By George, sir! I like a fellow who can take his life in his fist, as you've done—and none the worse if he bring a kind heart out of the tussle. My doctor's on the sick list. Will you take his place for the run to Suez? I'll enter you on the ship's books and give you berth aft?

DEX. I'm your man! My traps won't take much shifting. About my outfit, though? (*looking at his coat*) Seedy, ain't it? I've some old acquaintance aft here.

SMART. Never fear. We'll new rig you among us. Eh, Hardisty?

HARD. You're welcome to anything in my chest.

DEX. Spoken like a man and a brother!

Enter CAPTAIN CLAVERING, D. F. C. *He goes to* MISS COLEPEPPER'S *cabin, and knocks,* 2 E. R.

Oh! I've seen that face before. To be sure ; it's Clavering—one of my old Simla acquaintances.

CLAVERING *at* MISS COLEPEPPER'S *cabin.*

CLAVER. Miss Colepepper, your father has sent me to beg you'll come on deck. They've caught a shark.

SMART (*to* HARDISTY). Jump up, Hardisty, and see none of the people get their legs broken skylarking with the brute's tail.

[*Exit* HARDISTY, D. R. C.

DEX. (*coming towards* CLAVERING). Captain Clavering, I think ?

CLAVER. (*coldly and insolently*). Ya—a—a—s. (*staring at him.*)

DEX. You ought to remember me.

CLAVER. Ought I ? I don't though. (*turns on his heel.*)

Enter MISS COLEPEPPER, D. 2 E. R.

MISS C. I'm quite ready. (*sees* DEXTER *and recognizes him but half doubtfully*)

DEX. Yes, Miss Colepepper, you're quite right ; it is your old Badgerypore acquaintance.

MISS C. Mr. Dexter ! I did not know you were on board ; we have not seen you in the saloon.

DEX. No ! I'm in the steerage.

CLAVER. Captain Smart, I didn't know steerage passengers were admitted to the saloon.

SMART. This gentleman is one of my officers from to-day, Captain Clavering ; and my officers are company for my passengers.

CLAVER. Ah ! I say, Miss Colepepper, if you've any curiosity about the shark—(*goes up.*)

MISS C. Oh, yes,—(*to* DEXTER)—Mr. Dexter—(*embarassed*)—I am very glad to have met you ; I'm sure my father will have pleasure in renewing his acquaintance.

DEX. I don't think so or he'd not have left me to kick my heels among the Syces and Chuprassies under the verandah when I called at your house in Calcutta.

CLAVER, I say, Miss Colepepper, if you don't come the shark will be quite cut up. (*up stage.*)

DEX. Pray, go ; neither sharks nor staff-officers ought to be kept waiting.

MISS C. Come, Captain Clavering ; I'm very sorry, Mr. Dexter.

[*Exeunt* MISS COLEPEPPER *and* CAPTAIN CLAVERING, D. R.

SMART. Hang these young puppies of soldiers !

DEX. Never mind, Captain ; give me five minutes to freshen his memory, and I'll make this youngster civil enough, I'll answer for it. Come along ; only let me mount the P. and O. uniform. No man ever yet did justice to himself in a coat out at elbows.

[*Exit* DEXTER *and* SMART, R. C. D.

Enter MRS. SEBRIGHT *and* MRS. LOVIBOND, L. C. D.

MRS. S. (R.). No. I can't stand it. Catching the shark was all very good fun, but cutting him up—oh !

MRS. L. (L.). Ah ! Only think, my dear Mrs. Sebright, what that odious Mrs. Chatterly said of you just now ?

MRS. S. What did she say ?

MRS. L. That you had a natural sympathy with hooking——

Mrs. S. I'm very much obliged to her, poor dear! I've heard that sharks will take any bait. But I don't think Mrs. Chatterly would attract even a shark!

Mrs. L. A mere scrag of a woman, isn't she?

Mrs. S. Yes, like all Maypoles, can't bear anybody with a figure! Perhaps you heard that spiteful question she asked Captain Smart about you at dinner, yesterday — "whether Mrs. Lovibond paid for *two* berths?"

Mrs. L. Ah, my dear, people will say ill-natured things.

Mrs. S. And people will be so good natured in repeating 'em.

Mrs. L. It's a duty one owes one's friends—especially aboard ship! I assure you if I were to repeat half of what I heard said of you——

Mrs. S. Do pray let me hear! I do so delight in candid criticism?

Mrs. L. Then—they say you're a dreadful flirt—and that you're trying to get two strings to your bow—Sir Solomon and Mr. Colepepper. But that aiming at two birds generally succeeds in bagging neither.

Mrs. S. Now, only think how spiteful some people are. They say *you* would be glad of my leavings.

Mrs L. Oh! no, my dear. I have no ambition to have a pompous old fool like Sir Solomon, or a positive sexagenarian like Mr. Colepepper. Really, my dear,—if I might take the liberty of a friend——

Mrs. S. Do—pray do. If one's friends can't take liberties, who is to do it?

Mrs. L. I should advise you to be a leetle more on your guard—not to walk on deck quite so late in the evening—to be a leetle less demonstrative at dinner, and not to insist upon quite so many attentions from quite so many gentlemen. It makes other women jealous, you know. Not that I feel anything of the kind.

Mrs. S. Oh, dear, no! I'm sure, my dear Mrs. Lovibond, you must be quite satisfied with your monopoly of the major. So pleasant, after all the trouble you've had!

Mrs. L. Trouble, my love?

Mrs. S. In bringing such a stubborn wretch to your feet—in spite of *all* his resistance. I'm so glad you've succeeded! for I like you very much, you know.

Mrs. L. Not half so much as I like you.

Mrs. S. Never thought I could have been as fond of one so much older than myself.

Mrs. L. I assure you, I'm quite astonished to find myself overlooking in your case; so much that most people would call giddiness—if not levity.

Mrs. S. You are too kind, I'm sure, with the help of *your* experience.

Mrs. L. Oh! I'm afraid I must go to school to *you*—though you may be a year or two my junior.

Mrs. S. Dear me! is it possible you're only twenty-seven? How the Indian climate does tell on the constitution!

Mrs. L. It has one quality to recommend it to some people. . It makes a great many young widows. By-the-bye, do you know I've heard some censorious people on board wonder you don't wear your weeds.

Mrs S. How very odd! I've been bored to death with questions about the late Mr. Lovibond. (*confusion heard without, and cry, "man overboard."*)

Mrs. L What's that? Oh! gracious!

Mrs. S. A man overboard!

Enter Capt. Clavering, R. D. C., *supporting* Miss Colepepper, *who is fainting.*

CLAVER. Ya—as—a fellow tumbled from the main yard, and Miss Colepepper went off as if she'd been shot.

MRS. S. We'll attend to her. You run and learn the fate of the poor sailor.

CLAVER. I suppose the fellow can swim? Of course, everybody can swim. But I'll let you know.   [*Exit*, R. D. C.

MISS C. (*reviving*). Stay! Harry—Captain Clavering. Oh, if he should risk his life to save the drowning man.

MRS. S. I don't think he looks the least like it, my dear. (*cry without* —"*He's in—Huzza—huzza.*")

MRS. L. Hark! a splash! Somebody has jumped in! Oh! who is it?

Enter TOTTLE, R. D.

TOT. One of the officers! Where's the brandy?
          [*Exit, getting brandy bottle off* c. *table.*

MISS C. The officers! Should it be Clavering!

MRS. L. Oh! if it were my Hector! (*cries,* "*He's got him!*" "*He's down!*" "*No! here he is!*")

MRS. S. I'm very sorry—but I can't get up the slightest excitement. I'm certain it isn't Sir Solomon or Mr. Colepepper!

MISS C. This suspense is agony! (*sinks into a seat.*)

MRS. L. Oh! I can't bear it! (*imitating* MISS COLEPEPPER.)

MRS. S. Mind! It's no use you both fainting. I can only attend to one at a time! (*cries without—*"*Huzza—huzza.*")

Enter MAJOR McTURK, L. C. D.

MRS. S. (*screams.*)

McT. Clarinda! Don't be alarmed, ladies. I've saved 'em.

MISS C. You?

MRS. L. I knew he had! Oh! my noble Hector! (*rushes into his arms.*)

MISS C. Then it wasn't Captain Clavering?

McT. Clavering! Pooh! Before he had got his eyeglass screwed to a focus, I had rushed to the stern—sprang to the taffrail——

MRS. L. Precipitated yourself into the sea?

McT. No; not myself—the lifebuoy. They *said* they didn't want it! I knew better!

MISS C. They—who?

McT. Why, the man who fell overboard, and the fellow who went in after him——

MRS. S. Oh, then, there was somebody who threw *himself* into the sea, instead of the lifebuoy.

McT. Yes. Saw him go in from the main chains. A shabby genteel person—looked like a steerage passenger.

MISS C. And you don't know his name?

McT. Haven't the slightest idea!

MISS C. Shabby genteel heroism, it seems, must be content to be anonymous.

Enter SIR SOLOMON, R. H. D., *down* R. *of* MRS. SEBRIGHT.

MRS. S. But we heard it was one of the officers.

SIR S. One of the ship's officers, ladies. If they had only listened to me, I recommended flinging spars to leeward, or bringing up the ship in the wind and lowering a boat, at the same time pointing out to the captain the Company's reprehensible neglect in not having the vessel furnished with Clifford's patent boat lowering apparatus, which I shall feel it my duty to represent in the proper quarter.

MRS. S. And while you were talking this hasty person actually jumped overboard?

SIR S. In the most reckless manner! and so risked two lives instead of one.

Enter DEXTER, L. H. D., in uniform.

DEX. (*down* L. *of* MRS. SEBRIGHT). It's all right, ladies. The man's come to—thanks to hot gruel and blankets.

MISS C. And his gallant preserver?

DEX. Oh! he's none the worse for his ducking.

MISS C. But his name?

McT. If you insist on knowing, I can send my orderly to inquire in the steerage?

DEX. You may save yourself the trouble, Major. It was I jumped after the man.

MISS C. You, Mr. Dexter?

SIR S. Dexter—Dexter—I know that name I think.

DEX. I was medical adviser to the Nawaub of Ramshecklegur, while you were resident at his court, Sir Solomon.

SIR S. To be sure! Let me tell you, sir, your jumping overboard was a very rash and reprehensible act! If you had only reflected——

DEX. The man would have been drowned.

McT. Ah! if it hadn't been for the lifebuoy which I flung over——

DEX. Which I didn't avail myself of. Much obliged to *you*, all the same!

SIR S. (*aside*). Colepepper's engaged with the shark. Mrs. Sebright, (*offering his arm, up* R.) we're just passing Mocha. If you would like to know the statistics of our coffee trade with that region?

MRS. S. (*takes his arm*). Oh! delightful! I do so thirst for useful information!

[*Exit*, R. C., MRS. SEBRIGHT *and* SIR SOLOMON, *arm in arm.*

MRS. L. (*aside*). Especially from a K. C. B.

McT. (*to* MRS. LOVIBOND). Suppose we take a turn on deck! I have something very particular to communicate.

MRS. L. With pleasure, Major! Your conversation is always so instructive.

McT. You are such a *little* flatterer.

[*Exit* MRS. LOVIBOND, D. C. L., *and the* MAJOR.

DEX. (L. C.). Now we're alone, Miss Colepepper, let me hand over something of yours—which I have not had an earlier opportunity of returning. (*gives bracelet.*)

MISS C. The bracelet I lost that dreadful night the mutineers broke into our bungalow. The last thing I remember was a huge sowar—tearing it from my arm. How did you recover it?

DEX. Oh, the fellow was cut down. I picked up his booty as we carried you into the compound.

MISS C. Then you were there!—you saved me!

Enter CLAVERING, R. H. D., down R.

MISS C. Captain Clavering, I have at last discovered my preserver from the mutineers.

CLAVER. Indeed!

MISS. C. Let me introduce you to him. Mr. Dexter, Captain Clavering. (*goes up*—CLAVERING *bows haughtily.*)

Dex. I think Captain Clavering and I have met already.

Claver. I really can't remember it.

Dex. Can't you? It was at a whist party in the club-room, at Simla. The night of the 16th of August. You may remember, there was a little row about a missing——

Claver. (*embarrassed*). Ah—yes—I recall you perfectly now—Mr. Dexter, how do you do?—I am very glad to renew an acquaintance which——

Dex. Begun so very pleasantly.

Miss C. I must find my father, Captain Clavering; I want to tell him what we owe Mr. Dexter.

Dex. Pray oblige me by saying nothing about it. Like most Englishmen in the mutiny, I did my duty; but I really don't deserve any credit for it.

Miss C. (*aside*). As modest as he is brave. I will respect your generous wish, Mr. Dexter.

Claver. I hope you and I shall often meet, Mr. Dexter—it will give me the greatest pleasure. (*aside*) Confound his brazen face!

[*Exeunt* Miss Colepepper *and* Captain Clavering, R. C., *to the deck.*

Dex. There's one swell brought to his bearings for the rest of the voyage. It's *possible* the captain might have known nothing about that missing card—but when a fellow holds three honors for four deals runing, and has a trick of turning up aces——

Enter Captain Smart, R. H. C.

Smart. You're wanted, Doctor, in the forecastle. The man you saved insists on thanking you.

Dex. I'm glad *he* doesn't consider my jumping after him so very rash and reprehensible. He isn't a diplomatist.

Exeunt Dexter *and* Smart, D. R. C.

Enter Mrs. Lovibond, D. L. C., *sits in chair*, L. C.

Mrs. L. A declaration from the Major at last! I've been expecting it all the way from Madras—and yet, when it does come, how it flutters one! Three hundred a year, besides his pay. The man is a little pompous certainly, and not handsome. But then one has no right to be particular after thirty. I've asked time to consider his offer. First, am I a widow? I've every reason to think so. I have passed for one during the time I have been in India. It's now ten years since Mr. Lovibond left me, and since then no news of him but this melancholy letter. (*takes out a worn letter*) How often I've re-read it—" Clarinda—Meek as I am—much I have loved you—I write this to bid you farewell forever. If you should hear of an inquest on my remains, know that it is your jealousy and imperious disposition which have brought me to an untimely end. If ever you marry again, may you treat your second husband better than you have treated your long suffering, but to the last affectionate—Augustus." No date—a black edged envelope and the Dover postmark. I never *did* hear of an inquest—but I have always had poor Lovibond's untimely end upon my conscience. Let me endeavor to expiate my harshness to him by being all meekness and indulgence to his successor. I certainly do not feel that ardent attachment for the Major which young women think necessary for marriage. But do I care for him enough to make him happy? and myself, too, for that matter. That's a point I must settle, after mature deliberation—face to face with my dressing glass.   [*Exit into her cabin*, E. L.

Mrs. R. (*speaking to* Ayah *at the door of cabin*, U. E. R.). Remember, Sabrina—you will insist on the doctor coming to my babies directly.

2d Ayah. Yess, Missy Rabbits. [*Exit*, R. C.

Re-enter Mrs. Rabbits, *into cabin* 4, E. R. *Enter* Sir Solomon *and* Mrs. Sebright, D. L. C.

Mrs. S. (L.). And so these are really the waters where pearls come from?

Sir S. (R.). Yes. The trade is a considerable one—employs—let me see—about 10,000 tons of small craft and a capital of——

Mrs. S. Oh, I don't mind the figures. It's the lovely pearls I'm interested about! How I should like a handsome young diver to fish me up the finest set ever seen—bracelets, brooch, and bandeau—representing not so many pounds paid—but so many risks of life and limb—and all defied for me!

Sir S. But why sigh for pearls—when diamonds are within your reach?

Mrs. S. Diamonds, Sir Solomon?

Sir S. Yes. I flatter myself that Lady Fraser's diamonds will make a sensation at the drawing-room. What do you think of this as a specimen? (*produces case and shows diamond necklace.*)

Mrs. S. Oh! what a love of a necklace!

Sir S. And what a necklace for a love—for *my* love, my dear Mrs. Sebright—for *you*, if you will but say one little word! (*she is going to return the case*) No; don't pain me by refusing 'em.

Mrs S. But, Sir Solomon——

Sir S. I leave you till this evening to consider your ultimatum. Haste is always undesirable—whether in love or diplomacy (*aside*) There—I flatter myself that clinches old Colepepper. [*Exit*, R. C.

Mrs. S. To have been within an ace of a title and diamonds like these. Oh, dear—oh, dear! If only I weren't married already. John Sebright never gave me any diamonds! And I should look so well in 'em, I'm sure—(*puts them round her arm and turns it admiringly*) The very things for my complexion.

Enter Dexter, D. L. C.

I suppose Sir Solomon don't mean me to keep them—unless I take him into the bargain. To think the pompous, empty-headed creature should be allowed to tempt poor spinsters into his toils with such baits as these! Oh! you beauties! (*examines them in various lights.*)

Dex. (*aside*). Hollo! Why that's the identical necklace the Begum of Ramshacklegur offered me to poison the Nawaub! How can *she* have come by it! (*coming forward*) Magnificent!

Mrs. S. Oh, sir, you quite startled me!

Dex. I don't wonder at your being absorbed. I would recommend you not to show it on board, (*points to necklace*) or I wouldn't answer for your life among so many ladies.

Mrs. S. Oh, the necklace isn't mine! That is—if I can persuade Sir Solomon to take it back.

Dex. Sir Solomon—oh, ho—I'll save you all trouble on that point. (*takes it out of her hand and pockets it.*)

Mrs. S. (*offended*). Really, sir! This liberty from a perfect stranger.

Dex. Perhaps, to you; but, as an old friend of John Sebright's, I mustn't allow John Sebright's wife to expose herself to misconstruction.

Mrs. S. A friend of my husband's! Oh, sir!—how strange you must have thought it to see me passing as a widow!

Dex. Well—I don't think my friend John would quite like it.

Mrs. S. Oh, yes, he would! He always likes to see his little woman petted. You know, a prudent married woman without her husband has no chance aboard these horrid P. and O. boats! But a widow's always sure of attentions. Mind—I never said I was one—please don't betray me, Mr. Dexter. It's only till we reach Suez—there I'm to meet Jack—and I shan't want any attentions after that. Bless him!

Dex. Attentions are one thing—diamonds are another. I shall return these to Sir Solomon.

Mrs. S. I'm afraid he'll be very angry.

Dex. I'll pacify him.

Mrs. S. But what shall I say when he comes for his answer and his necklace ?

Dex. For his necklace refer him to me. For his answer—say that you've a husband already—one of the best fellows in the world, and that you're heartily ashamed of yourself for not having told him so ten days ago.

Mrs. S. Oh, dear—oh, dear—I shall look so ridiculous!

Dex. If you don't like telling the truth, you must invent fibs for yourself—only remember there's a friend of John Sebright's on board to look after John Sebright's wife.

Mrs. S. John Sebright's wife will look after herself, Mr. Dexter! (*crosses to* L.)

Dex. Bravo! I like that little bit of flare-up better than anything you've said yet! Excuse me—I've some patients to attend to.

[*Exit into* Mrs. Rabbits' *cabin*, R., *No.* 4.

Mrs. S. Patients, indeed! He shan't find me among his patients, I can tell him! How dare he talk in that way! as if I were behaving in a manner my dear Jack wouldn't approve! What harm can there be in accepting all the attentions one can get? Aboard ship, too, where everybody's so selfish! If he weren't a man, I might be sure it must be all jealousy—but he doesn't care for me! He can't be jealous. It's provoking to be so misconstrued—and by a friend of dear Jack's, too—shall I do as he told me ? Tell Sir Solomon and Mr. Colepepper that I'm a married woman? They'll say I've made fools of them both. I shall be talked about all over the ship—and if I say nothing about my husband, when Jack meets me at Suez who knows what people may tell *him!* Oh! I wish I had never allowed anybody to pay me any attentions! I wish I had bored everybody to death about my husband the first day I came on board. I wish—I wish - (*passionately*)—Oh, I wish I were at the bottom of the sea! [*Exit into her cabin,* 1, E. R.

Lovibond (*from his cabin, No.* 2, L.). Steward! steward! I say, steward! (*the door of* Lovibond's *cabin,* 2. E L., *opens, and* Lovibond *looks hastily out. He wears a white cotton nightcap, a long white flannel dressing-gown, and is endeavoring, with a towel, to staunch the blood from a cut he has given himself in shaving—comes forward calling "steward"*) I was tormented all yesterday by an individual answering to that name, who kept harping on the disgusting subject of dinner; (*shudders*) and now that I really want him—of course he's not to be found! I wish I could get some sticking plaster. (*shows cut on his jaw*) This is the sanguinary consequence of trying to shave one's self—under the mingled effects of vertigo and a swing-glass. I thought myself uncommonly lucky to secure a passage at Aden by taking Mr. Downy's berth off his hands. How I exulted over the dozen parties who names stood on the P. and O. books before Augustus Lovibond's. What would I have given to have changed places with them yesterday! The agonies I've suffered in the last twenty-four hours on that layer of hard substance which they call a bed—in that elevated coffin, which they call a berth. The shiver of the screw, and the gnawing of the timbers, and the clashing of the chains overhead; and the pitching and the tossing; and, worse than all, the rattle of knives and forks out here, and the notion that eating was going on within arm's length of my—(*turns sick*) I feel a leetle (*smiling*) better this morning. But my head still seems to be set on a pivot. However, let me console myself with the reflection that I'm on my way home to England after nine years broiling at Singapore. I never could have endured my exile, but that England meant Clarinda and the chains of matrimony. But it's now three years since she left London for India. Let's hope she has found another victim by this time. She could do it legally, I believe, after hearing nothing of me for seven years, even if my parting letter hadn't convinced her I was no more. Well, if she *has* married again, I wish her husband joy of her. What a temper that woman had! Oh! good heavens, what a temper to be sure! Even a Singapore sun was better than the perpetual domestic broil I endured with Mrs. Lovibond. (*door of* Mrs. Rabbits' *cabin opens.*)

Dex. (*without*). The pills at bedtime, my dear madam. The draught in the morning.

. Lov. Passengers coming this way! Good gracious! I'm not fit to be seen in this pickle! Which is my cabin? Confound it! all the doors are alike—and my head's in such a whirl! This is it, I think.

[*Exit into* Mrs. Lovibond's *cabin*, 1 e. l.

Mrs. R. I shall attend most carefully to your directions, doctor. (*a shriek heard from* Mrs. Lovibond's *cabin*. Mrs. Rabbits *and* Dexter *appear on the threshold of the cabin*) Hark! what's that?

Dex. A squall! (*they pause.*)

Lovibond *hastily re-enters.*

Lov. The wrong cabin, by jingo! I've frightened some unfortunate female into hysterics. Eh—this must be my door. My head is in such a whirl!   [*Exit into his own cabin*, 2 e. l.

Mrs. R. Doctor, did you see that?

Enter McTurk, d. l. c.

Dex. A man in a dressing gown bolting into cabin No. 2.

Mrs. R. Coming out of cabin No. 1—and cabin No. 1 is Mrs. Lovibond's!

. McT. A man coming out of Clarinda's cabin! (*coming forward*) What's that you say, madam?

Mrs. R. What I blush to repeat, major. The doctor and I have just seen a gentleman leaving Mrs. Lovibond's cabin—I repeat, a gentleman —and in a dressing gown! Imagine my feelings—the feelings of a virtuous mother of a numerous family. I will not trust myself to dwell upon the subject! (*re-enters her cabin*, u. e. r., *with dignity.*)

McT. Is this true, sir?

Dex. I can't deny the fact—but it may have a great many explanations.

McT. Explanations! Don't talk to me, sir! Hector McTurk is not to be humbugged, sir! The individual who left that cabin visited it either by Mrs. Lovibond's invitation, or forced his way into it against her will. In either case he must settle accounts with Hector McTurk. I'll blow out any man's brains who presumes to love Clarinda Lovibond! and as for the man who dares to insult her—I'll——

Dex. You can't well do more for him, major. Come, it may have been only a mistake. I'll keep Mrs. Rabbits quiet, if you'll promise not to say anything to Mrs. Lovibond till I've made inquiries.

McT. Till then, doctor, I'll bottle up my feelings. It's right you should know I've just proposed to Mrs. Lovibond! and better cross the path of the man-eater in his hunger, than come betwen Hector McTurk and the object of his preference.   [*Exit*, L. D. C.

DEX. If the lion's skin only made the lion, Hector McTurk is a very formidable personage.

MRS. L. (*without, in a faint voice*). Ayah—Mrs. Grimwood—would anybody be good enough to go for the doctor!

DEX. The doctor is here, my dear madam. (*knocks.*)

Enter MRS. LOVIBOND, *very pale and agitated.*

MRS. L. Oh, doctor—answer me one question. Do you believe in ghosts?

DEX. Ghosts generally resolve themselves, in medical opinion, into delirium tremens, or deranged liver.

MRS. L. Oh—but seriously, doctor—do you believe the spirits of the departed are ever allowed to revisit this world?

DEX. Allow me. (*feels her pulse*) As I suspected. Quick and throbby—let me recommend a calmant.

MRS. L. This is no case for medicine. Listen, doctor—I'm not insane—I'm in perfect health—but not five minutes ago—in that cabin—I saw the spirit of *my* late husband.

DEX. A spirit!

MRS. L. Arrayed in the habilliments of the grave—a yawning wound in his throat—oh, horrible! We were unhappy together—I was the cause. He left me with a threat of self-destruction—I have reason to believe he fell by his own hand—I was on the point of accepting a second husband. The spirit of my poor Augustus must have been sent to warn or deter me.

DEX. Calm yourself, my dear lady. Some one may have entered your cabin by mistake—whom your imagination invested with these ghostly attributes. I may succeed in satisfying you of this. Meanwhile, I'll send you a composing draught. For whom shall I say?

MRS. L. Mrs. Lovibond—No. 1.

DEX. Very good. You had better take care of No. 1, and keep yourself quiet for the present.

MRS. L. I will try—but I almost dread to re-enter this cabin.

DEX. Never fear, madam. The ghost won't show himself while I'm here. They have a horror of doctors. (*Exit* MRS. LOVIBOND *into cabin No.* 1.) Ah, ah, ah! A ghost in a white cotton night cap!

LOV. (*puts out his head*). I really must find some sticking plaster.

DEX. The ghost, for a pony! Ha, ha, ha!

LOV. That's a very lively person. I beg your pardon, sir, but have you such a thing as a piece of court plaster about you?

DEX. (*takes out case*). Here you are, sir—black, white, or flesh colored. Which would you prefer?

LOV. Well, I think black the most becoming. (*licks it and tries to stick it on*) Oh, dear, I haven't lick'd the gummy side——

DEX. Cut yourself in shaving, I see—I'm the ship's surgeon—allow me. (*puts on the piece of plaster*) The yawning gash in the throat! Ha, ha, ha!

LOV. Really, sir—my wound may not be exactly serious. But I'm not aware that it's a fit subject for ridicule.

DEX. Excuse me, sir; but the lady whose cabin you entered just now——

LOV. By mistake, I assure you, sir. My brain's in such a topsy-turvey state; I'm quite incapable of such an'intrusion intentionally.

DEX. I can quite believe it—especially in your present costume. But that lady——

LOV. I'm quite ready to make her the most ample apology, in writing, if necessary. If you'd oblige me with her name.

DEX. Mrs. Lovibond!

LOV. (aghast). Eh! Mrs. Lovibond?

DEX. Yes. Only fancy—she took you for the ghost of her late husband! Ha, ha, ha!

LOV. (with a ghastly attempt at laughter). Ha, ha, ha!

DEX. And while she takes you for a ghost, Major McTurk—who it seems, has just proposed to her—is determined to make you one.

LOV. Eh? Major McTurk has just proposed to Claria—to that lady?

DEX. Yes, and means to blow out your brains. He interprets your visit to Mrs. Lovibond's cabin as the triumph of a rival—or the intrusion of a daring libertine.

LOV. My dear, sir, I'm not a daring libertine. Do I look like one? I'm anything but that, I assure you.

Enter MOLESKIN, *behind from* L. C.

Tell him—tell everybody—that my name is Downy—a respectable merchant of Singapore—that I'm dreadfully ill—unable to leave my cabin —I promise you I won't show my nose outside of it, till we're safe at Suez.

DEX Oh, you'll be all right in a day or two.

LOV. I don't want to be all right in a day or two—I've the best reasons for keeping myself to myself—I hate strangers—I detest society— I'm a regular misanthrope, however little you might think so to look at me—oh, sir—if you want to save a fellow creature from the most painful consequences, help to keep up my incognito—promise me! If money can bind you to secrecy——

DEX. Not the least occasion for that. We doctors are the best father confessors. Heaven bless a good many of our patients if we weren't!

LOV. Ah, sir, you've taken a load off my mind. I'm quite happy— that is—I should be—if my cabin was only a little less crowded with luggage. (aside) I've half of Downy's, as well as my own. If you only get a little of it cleared away I should think it a perfect paradise of eight feet by ten.

DEX. I'll send the steward to clear away some of your traps. (crosses L., and looks into LOVIBOND'S cabin.)

LOV. The fact is, I'd rather not see anybody—not even the steward.

DEX. (looking into the cabin No. 2). Why, you've luggage enough for a lady. (goes to cabin No. 2 and looks into it.)

LOV. (aside, while DEXTER examines luggage). My wife only separated from me by a slight partition! This major thirsting for my blood! Here's a situation on the edge of two volcanoes, and sea-sick into the bargain. How lucky I'm down on the passengers' list under the name of Downy. (re-enters cabin No. 2.)

DEX. (coming out of cabin No 2). What the deuce can the poor devil be afraid of? I suppose it's the fire-eating major.

MOLE. (coming down, L. H.). Doctor, I hope you respect the laws of your country.

DEX. Yes, in a general way.

MOLE. You ain't aiding, abetting, and comforting him, are you?

DEX. Him? Who?

MOLE. This here Downy—the party occupying this here cabin. The party that hates society—society returns the compliment, I can tell him.

LOV. (*within*). Here's a bag I can very well spare, doctor; and a hat box I don't want. Oh! and here's a portmanteau that's always getting between my legs. (*puts a portmanteau, hat case, black bag, etc., outside of door.*)

MOLE. (*seizes bag*). The very identical bag named in my instructions! (*he proceeds to pick the lock.*)

DEX. Hollo! what are you at?

MOLE. Identifying—(*takes out papers*) all right. The missing securities —the forged bills—everything but the specie.

Enter SMART, D. R. H., *down* C.

DEX. Here, captain, bear a hand to stop this.

SMART. What's the row? (*comes forward.*)

DEX. Lunacy or larceny—rifling a passenger's luggage!

MOLE. It's all right, gentlemen—I'm a detective. In the Queen's name, I charge you to aid me in arresting Thomas Downy, alias, etc., etc., etc., charged in this warrant with fraudulent bankruptcy, forgery, and felony (*producing warrant*) at Colombo.

SMART (*looks at warrant*). A felon aboard my ship!

DEX. My friend the ghost! This explains his anxiety about his incognito.

MOLE. Now mind, gentlemen, I look to you to help me. This here Downy's a desperate character—it's probable he'll resist. But the warrant's all regular; so if he kills any of us it'll be murder.

DEX That's a comfort!

MOLE. Call him, doctor—he'll come out to you.

DEX. Poor devil!—but after all one mustn't pity a felon. (*knocks*) Mr. Downy.

LOV. (*within*). Yes, doctor.

DEX. (L.). Come out, I want to speak to you.

Enter LOVIBOND.

LOV. Strangers! Oh, doctor, is this your fidelity?

MOLE. (*laying his hand on his shoulder and handcuffing him*). Thomas Downy, I arrest you as a felon in the Queen's name!

LOV. Me—stop—this is a mistake.

MOLE. Is it?

LOV. My name's not Downy—no—yes—it ain't. Oh! gracious! (*falls into chair*, C.)

Tableau.

ACT II.

SCENE.—*The poop deck of the Simoon, towards evening ; groups of passengers seen sitting and walking ; four* MUSICIANS *playing the end of an overture up* L. MRS. SEBRIGHT *and* COLEPEPPER *discovered, she seated in a lounging chair,* L. C., *he seated on her* R.—*a* KHITMAGAR *in attendance up* L. SIR SOLOMON (*smoking a cigar on one of the seats,* R. C., *round the skylight) watching them, while he pretends to read.*

MRS. S. (*reading from "Don Juan," after music has ceased*).
       "They look'd up to the sky, whose floating glow
            Spread like a rosy ocean, vast and bright ;
       They gazed upon the glittering sea below,
            Whence the broad moon rose circling into sight ,
       They heard the waves splash, and the winds so low,
            And saw each other's dark eyes darting light
                 Into each other——"
(*she stops, and is about to shut the book*) That's quite enough !
   COLE. (*taking the book*). No ; let me finish the stanza, my dear Mrs. Sebright—(*he reads*)
                 " And, beholding this,
       Their lips·drew nearer and clung unto."
   MRS. S. (*shivering*). Oh, I'm so cold !
   COLE. Good heavens ! and you're not half wrapped up. (*to* L.) Qui-hi ! —(KHITMAGAR *approaches down* L. *and salaams*—COLEPEPPER *whispers*—KHITMAGAR *salaams and exits by companion,* L. H.) The evenings are positively chilly. I've sent my Khitmagar for another shawl.
   MRS. S. You're very kind, I'm sure. I'm quite ashamed to give you so much trouble ; but it's very pleasant to be so devotedly waited on.
   COLE. The pleasure is entirely on the side of your attendant, my dear Mrs. Sebright. Ah ! when will you give me right to offer you a life-long attention ?

Re-enter KHITMAGAR *from below with handsome Indian shawl.* COLEPEPPER *takes shawl from* KHITMAGAR, *who exits,* L.

Allow me.
   MRS. S. Oh, what a splendid Cashmere ! (*drapes herself in it.*)
                 [*One* LADY *and* GENTLEMEN *rise and exit,* L.
   COLE. It was never properly displayed till now. These shoulders are too lovely for any less costly drapery.
   MRS. S. Oh dear ! Oh dear ! Really, Mr. Colepepper, you shouldn't show a poor weak woman such things. How is one to resist them ?
   COLE. Let me hope you will continue to wear it by the best title—as—
   MRS. S. (*hastily rising*). Hadn't we better take a turn about the deck ? I should never forgive myself if you caught a chill.
   COLE. Pooh, pooh ! my dear lady, I've an iron constitution ; I'm no molly-coddle like Sir Solomon yonder. But if you prefer walking, I'm at your service. (*they walk up arm-in-arm,* L. H.)
   SIR S. (*comes forward* R.). It's astonishing how that old man can make such an ass of himself. I wonder Mrs. Sebright can tolerate his anti-quated attentions. And that shawl, too ! I flatter myself my necklace will take the shine out of his old-fashioned Cashmere !

Enter Dexter *from the companion,* R. H.

Ah, Dexter! Delicious evening. Allow me to offer you a cheroot. (*presents his case.*

Dex. Thank you. (*lights cheroot—throws himself on* Mrs. Sebright's *chair,* L. c.) A sunset sky—a sea breeze—an easy chair—and a prime cheroot—I call this paradise.

Sir S. (*sits* R. H.). With a superbundance of Eves, doctor.

Dex. (*nodding towards* Mrs. Sebight). Yonder goes one, at all events, with her old serpent at her side.

Sir S. Colepepper, eh? A capital simile. Why, it's not five minutes since he tempted her with that shawl she's displaying so coquettishly.

Dex. Poor May! Roguish old January! (*puffs a whiff of smoke*)

Sir S. A charming person, Mrs. Sebright—a leetle too fond of attentions, perhaps.

Dex. "A leetle," without the "perhaps."

Sir S. It's melancholy to see her listening to the antediluvian gallantries of an old scarecrow like Colepepper, so young as she is.

Dex. A mere child.

Sir S. So inexperienced!

Dex. Innocence itself!

Sir S. You know her, I think.

Dex. Oh, yes; we're old acquaintances.

Sir S. It would be a charity to open her eyes to the absurdity of Mr. Colepepper's attentions—he's sixty-four, if he's a day.

Dex. Really!

Sir S. Hasn't a square inch of sound liver left, and no more calf to his leg than my walking stick.

Dex. Then he makes up uncommonly well.

Sir S. Wadding, Dexter; all wadding! And then, his temper! —simply de-testable! He says he's going home on his pension; but, between ourselves, it's to make friends with the Council. There's a screw loose in his Badgerypore accounts—important vouchers missing. He says they were stolen in the mutiny.

Captain Clavering *and* Miss Colepepper *enter from* R. H. *and join* Mrs. Sebright.

Dex. (*aside*). That box of papers I secured. (*to* Sir S.) The Commissioner's bungalow *was* plundered, you know.

Sir S. Oh! of course. Depend upon it, the mutiny has been an uncommonly convenient event for a great many people.

Dex. Really, it would be a charity to put Mrs. Sebright up to all this.

Sir S. Well, if a friend could just hint the truth to her—not that I want to put a spoke in Colepepper's rusty old wheel——

Dex. Oh! every one who knows Sir Solomon Fraser must be aware of his disinterestedness.

Sir S. Yes, I've been a sufferer by it all my life; but it's constitutional, and, talking of constitutions, I don't think mine will be improved by this night air; I'll just get another wrapper. Meanwhile, if you should have an opportunity to put Mrs. Sebright on her guard——

Dex. Trust me to do justice to your hints, Sir Solomon.

Sir S. (*rising—aside*). Now I call that diplomatically managed. (*goes up, exit,* R. H.)

Dex. (*aside*). The rascally old backbiter wants me to play the cat to get *his* chestnuts out of the fire. (Mr. Colepepper *leaves the group and comes forward,* L. H.)

COLE. Good evening, Mr. Dexter! I'm very glad to have an opportunity of renewing our Badgerypore acquaintance. Though a civil servant,
I have never shrunk from intimacy with the press. Your way of con-
ducting your paper got you immense credit.

DEX Did it, Mr. Colcpepper ? I always found people eager for ready
money, notwithstanding.

COLE. I mean credit with the Governor General, and the authorities at
Calcutta. You set your brethren of the press an excellent example of
courage and straightforwardness—noble qualities, Mr. Dexter; noble
qualities, sir.

DEX. Then I wish the authorities had paid what I lost by them.

COLE. Ah, Mr. Dexter, such virtue, I'm afraid——

SIR SOLOMON *comes down* R. H., *and joins* MRS. SEBRIGHT.

DEX. Is it's own reward, Mr. Colepepper. I've been fully repaid in
that rather unsubstantial currency.

COLE. Oh, you would have triumphed over all difficulties, my dear sir,
if it hadn't been for the mutiny. We have all been sufferers by that
deplorable event—civil servants, soldiers, private adventurers, women.
Why, look at our passengers; observe the melancholy proportion of
widows!

DEX. Say, rather, the uncommonly jolly proportions of some of the
widows, my crummy friend—Mrs. Lovibond, for example.

COLE Or pretty little Mrs. Sebright yonder. (*aside*) Confound it!
there's Sir Solomon at her elbow. A charming woman, Mr. Dexter.

DEX. Very.

COLE. It's a pity she should get herself talked about with that pecu-
liarly silly old fellow, Fraser.

DEX. Sir Solomon is not the wisest of men, certainly; but he's a
K. C. B., Mr. Colepepper

COLE. Titles are empty things, Mr. Dexter.

DEX. And are often appropriately bestowed on empty people.

COLE. Too true. Sir Solomon is a melancholy example. Mrs. Sebright's friends ought really to open her eyes. She's much too interest-
ing a creature to be thrown away on a battered old beau like Sir
Solomon.

DEX. Old ? Why, he don't look above five-and-forty.

COLE. Art, Mr. Dexter, all art—cosmetics, hair dyes, false teeth.

DEX. What a very diplomatic *tout ensemble!* But are you positive
about the teeth ?

COLE. My Khitmagar caught his man cleaning 'em only the other
day. They're taken out at night and replaced in the morning, like his
shirt studs. Then, as for his diplomatic reputation, it's all a hollow
mockery, sir.

DEX. Like his teeth—eh ?

COLE. Exactly, and not quite so easily cleaned; for, between ourselves, there's an awkward charge hanging over him at this moment—of
taking "backsheesh" when resident at Ramshacklegur.

DEX. (*aside*). That accounts for the necklace.

COLE. You know, accepting presents by civil servants is against regu-
lations. If the charge is brought home to Sir Solomon he'll be disgraced
—of course, as a friend of his, I regret to hear such things; but one
can't quite shut one's ears, you know.

DEX. (*aside*). No, nor one's mouth neither.

SIR SOLOMON *is seen earnestly speaking to* MRS. SEBRIGHT—*they then separ-*

*ate—*Sir Solomon *crosses to* R *, converses with a lady—*Mrs. Sebright *down* L., *approaching* Dexter.

Cole. Now, it may be a melancholy duty to open her eyes, but they ought to be opened ; and if you should have an opportunity—there she comes ! Break it to her gently, my dear sir ; but, whatever you do, break it. *(aside)* Ehem ! I think I've out-manœuvered the diplomatist. *(goes up,* R. H., *by the opposite side to that by which* Mrs. Sebright *comes down,* L., *and rejoins his daughter and* Captain Clavering.)

Mrs. S. Oh, Mr. Dexter, I'm so glad to catch you at last alone. I thought that tiresome Mr. Colepepper would never have left you.

Dex. Don't say tiresome ; he was singing your praises. I conclude from that that you haven't told him the truth yet.

Mrs. S. About John ? *(hesitatingly)* No, not exactly.

Dex. Allow me to relieve you of *that* shawl. *(takes off the shawl* Colepepper *has given her—folds it up—puts it on seat,* C.)

Mrs. S. Mr. Dexter, how dare you take such a liberty ?

Dex. I want it to keep company with Sir Solomon's necklace. I suppose you haven't told him the truth, neither ?

Mrs. S. Not yet, Mr. Dexter ; you see it's so very awkward.

Dex. It always is awkward to get back to the hard road of facts from the soft but shifting sands of falsehood.

Mrs. S. Oh, if you only knew the perplexity I'm in ! They've both proposed. I tried everything to prevent it.

Dex. Everything but the truth.

Mrs. S. I'm sure I did my best. I flirted with Sir Solomon in hopes to drive away Mr. Colepepper ; and then I coquetted with Mr. Colepepper on purpose to disgust Sir Solomon. But it's all of no use ! I'm fairly at my wit's end.

Dex. Then, as wit's exhausted, you may as well fall back on wisdom ; and wisdom says, "Tell the truth and shame the devil." It must be done, and better out of your mouth than other people's. Suppose I helped you to a good reason for saying "No" to both of them ?

Mrs. S. Oh, I should be so thankful—that is, any reason but the real one.

Dex. Each is amiably anxious to save you from the other. According to Sir Solomon, Mr. Colepepper is sixty-five—worn out in constitution —damaged in reputation—and cloudy in prospects. If I may believe Mr. Colepepper, Sir Solomon is an empty, made-up coxcomb—with false hair—false complexion—false teeth—and factitious reputation— and with the sword of official disgrace hanging over him by a hair. Now, you have only to hold up to *each* of your admirers the picture of him painted by the *other*, to escape from both with flying colors. Come, you *must* get out of the scrape somehow. I've put the clue in your hand— follow it—at least it will lead you straight forward. Here comes Sir Solomon. *(crosses behind her, retires up to* L.)

Sir Solomon, *down* R.

Sir S. My dear Mrs. Sebright, the term for delivering your ultimatum has expired. You promised an answer to my proposal this evening.

Mrs. S. Really, Sir Solomon—I feel quite unworthy——

Sir S. Not unworthy. Beauty, youth, and grace have their claims, even against family, title, and diamonds.

Mrs. S. I'm very sorry—I'm afraid you will think me very ungrateful—but—in fact—there's an insurmountable obstacle.

Sir S. An obstacle ? You don't mean Mr. Colepepper ?

Mrs. S. Mr. Colepepper!—what an idea! Why, he's sixty-five, if he's a day—a ruined constitution—a bad temper—and anything but brilliant prospects.

Sir S. (*chuckling, aside*). Bravo! *my* thunder! Well, done, doctor! (Colepepper *comes down, L.*)

Mrs. S. No. I'm sure if there was nothing more formidable in your way than Mr. Colepepper——

Sir S. Here he comes. (*aside*) We must renew this conversation. She means to say yes, or she'd have returned the necklace. [*Retires up R.*]

Cole (*coming down L.*). My dear Mrs. Sebright, I've been grilling over a slow fire while Sir Solomon has been bestowing his tediousness upon you. I hope you have weighed my proposal.

Mrs. S. I'm sure, Mr. Colepepper, nothing would have given me greater pleasure, but——

Cole. "But!" Am I to understand there's a "but" in the way?

Mrs. S. I'm sorry to say there is—a very great "but."

Cole. I know who it is—that puppy, Sir Solomon!

Mrs. S. He is a "great butt," certainly; but you needn't be jealous of Sir Solomon—a battered old beau—vain—frivolous—with a made-up face—dyed hair—and false teeth!

Cole. (*aside*). Bravo! Exactly the points I put to Dexter! (Sir Solomon *comes-down R.*) Here he comes. We'll pursue our conversation by-and-bye. (*aside*) She seems to have packed up my shawl—that must mean accepting.

Sir S. Now, pray don't let me interrupt your tête-a-tête.

Cole. Not at all, Sir Solomon. (*bugle sounds, L.*) That's the supper bugle. Mrs. Sebright was just going down for a little refreshment. (*the groups on deck break up and descend the companions, and through the rail by the slips at back.*)

Mrs. S. May I trouble you to bring my things? (*they gather up shawls, footstool, etc. Aside*) How I wish I could get both off my hands! (*each approaches with his load on one arm, and offers her the other—go up talking—exeunt by companion, R.*)

Smart, (R.) Dexter, (C.) *and* Moleskin, (L.) *come forward from the rail.*

Mole. I put it to you, doctor, as a medical man, whether it ain't impossible for the prisoner to keep up his constitution in this 'ere climate, without fresh hair and *h*exercise?

Dex. He certainly would be all the better for "*fresh hair*," to judge by what I saw under his white cotton extinguisher. He ought to be trotted on deck at least a couple of hours every day.

Mole. So I tell him. "Look here, Mr. Downy," I says, "I don't want to have you die on my hands. The warrant charges me to take your body—but your dead body would be no manner of use." But he won't listen to *me*, bless you. There he sits, moping and maundering, and declaring he's somebody else.

Smart. I'm Captain, here. Come along with me, Mr. Moleskin, and I ll have him on deck, if I've to bouse him up by the skylight. But, remember, his arrest is to be kept quiet for the credit of the ship.

Mole. All right, Captain—mum as a mouse. Nobody needn't know anything but that we're friends—such very good friends, we can't loose sight o' one another.

Dex. But he can't run away from your custody here.

Enter Mrs. Lovibond *from companion, L.*

MOLE. How do I know what papers he may have stowed away ? If
I didn't keep a heye on him, he might throw 'em overboard, or himself
either—he's artful enough.

SMART. Well, come along, Mr. Moleskin. (MOLESKIN *crosses*) The deck's
all quiet now; we'll have him up in a jiffy. [*Exit* SMART *and* MOLESKIN, R.

MRS. L. (*coming forward*). Mr. Dexter, you know Major McTurk—may
I ask if he has confided to you the delicate relation in which we stand?

DEX. I am aware that the Major has popped—I beg your pardon—
proposed to you, and I applaud his taste.

MRS. L. Then perhaps he has also confided to you the reason of the
strange alteration in his manner since this morning—his coldness—his
estrangement?

DEX. Oh, yes ; it was the ghost. Ha, ha, ha !

MRS. L. Sir, that mysterious apparition is no subject for levity.

DEX. Mysterious! I wish all ghosts could be explained away so
easily ! It turns out that the supposed ghost was a sea-sick passenger,
which accounts for his cadaverous complexion ; his habiliments of the
grave resolve themselves into a white cotton nightcap and flannel dressing gown; and the yawning wound in his throat, was a cut he had
given himself in shaving—he had blundered into your cabin, and was
seen by the Major making his retreat.

MRS. L. Could the Major do me the injustice to suspect! But are
you sure it was a man?

DEX. "I'll take the ghost's word, for a thousand pounds !"—I had it
from his own lips.

MRS. L. But the extraordinary resemblance to my late husband ?

DEX. Accident, no doubt, or your fancy,

MRS. L. Do you know this intruder's name ?

DEX Downy.

MRS. L. Oh, what a ·relief! I expect the Major My dear doctor,
may I ask you to explain this to him, and spare me painful references
to the past ?

DEX. With pleasure. (MRS. LOVIBOND *retires*, L. H.) By Jove ! I'm
gradually becoming the pivot on which everything turns in this ship.
(MCTURK *comes up by the rail*, R. H.) I had·no notion a P. and O. doctor's
duty was to patch up more lover's quarrels than broken heads, and to
administer as many doses of calumny as of calomel. Both dangerous
medicines, and both a great deal too much resorted to. Well, Major, I
told you I should find an explanation of the intrusion on Mrs. Lovibond's
cabin this morning I've found it.

McT. Satisfactory ?

DEX. Perfectly. It turns out as I expected, that the intruder is an
entire stranger to the lady. Only came on board at Aden. He left his
cabin to call the steward, and was too sea-sick to find his way back
again.

McT. Oh, if you can satisfy me he was a stranger to Mrs. Lovibond,
I shall merely insist upon a public apology in the presence of all the
saloon passengers. But, mind, only if he's a stranger. Let me dis-
cover any intimacy between 'em, or even acquaintanceship, and, (*imi-
tates the action of firing a pistol*) one of us must fall—and I don't mean
it to be me. (MISS COLEPEPPER *comes up with a book and sits near the skylight*, R.) Supper will be over; aren't you coming down ?

DEX. No; I prefer solitude and a cigar. (*Exit*, MAJOR, R. *Aside*) There's
Mary Colepepper—she sees me. Will she speak ? I won't. If *she's* proud,
so am I ! (*smokes*—MISS COLEPEPPER, *after a pause and a moment's
hesitation, closes her book and approaches.*)

MISS C. Mr. Dexter! (*embarrassed.*)

DEX. Miss Colepepper a truant from the supper table!

MISS C. This lovely sea and sky have more attractions for me, I confess, than the saloon. (*both sit*, C.)

DEX. I am glad to find one person on board of my way of thinking. (*a pause*) I hope my cigar does not annoy you.

MISS C. Oh, no! I don't dislike it in the open air. (*another pause—she fumbles with the book—-he takes his cigar from his mouth—each is about to speak, but each, perceiving the other's intentions, pauses embarrassed.*)

DEX. I beg your pardon—did you speak?

MISS C. No; I thought you did.

DEX. No; but are you sure my smoke doesn't blow in your face? Perhaps I'd better shift to leward. (*rises as if to go across the deck.*)

MISS C. Don't stir on my account, pray. I am glad of an opportunity of expressing to you my gratitude for the preservation I owe to your courage on that terrible night of the mutiny; my admiration of the unselfish humanity with which you risked your life to-day, to save a poor sailor.

DEX. Miss Colepepper, take my advice, and never praise a man for doing his duty. It makes him uncomfortable when it does not make him conceited.

MISS C. At least let me express my regret that my father did not receive you with more hospitality at Calcutta. I'm sure if he had known all we owed you——

DEX. I didn't knock at your father's door as a creditor, but as an acquaintance. I ought to have remembered Calcutta wasn't Badgerypore, and the convenient newspaper editor an altogether different personage from the out-at-elbows tramp.

MISS C. But if you really knew my father, I am sure you would esteem, as well as like him. Long habits of authority have made him imperious and hasty—apt to stand on his dignity.

DEX. His dignity! You would, laugh, perhaps, to hear me talk of mine; but I *have* such a thing. The time may come when *your father* will be as frank in owning my services as *you* are now. I will accept his recognition from his own lips, but not by proxy from yours. Meantime, forgive me, if I measure our intimacy

Enter CLAVERING, R.

rather by what I know to be your father's notions of social etiquette than your kindly impulses. Here's Captain Clavering coming in search of you. *He's* up to the mark. There can be no impropriety in *his* acting as your escort, and if acquaintance with him should grow into a warmer feeling——(*both rise.*)

MISS C. Mr. Dexter! you have no right to suggest such a thing! Captain Clavering is an acquaintance of papa's—not of my choosing.

DEX. I beg your pardon, I was guilty of an impertinence; but it's difficult not to be bitter now and then, in spite of the most philosophic intentions.

CLAVERING, *down* R.

CLAVER. I come as a deputation to ask you if you will give us a little music down stairs? They want "La ci darem"—I'm ready to take the bass.

DEX. (*aside*). That I'll swear you are!

MISS C. I don't feel in voice this evening, Captain Clavering. (*turns away.*)

CLAVER. Now, really, that's very provoking! I'll tell 'em so. (*goes round to skylight,* L., *and speaks down as if to guests*) They'll all be in despair !

DEX. (*aside to* MISS COLEPEPPER). Not in voice ? Oh, Miss Colepepper! The tone in which you said "Captain Clavering," just now, was the pleasantest music I've heard for many a day. So delightfully chilling ! Do sing !

MISS C Not with him ! Will *you* sing with me ?

DEX. Will I not!

MISS C. Then I'll sing.

DEX. But you refused Clavering ?

MISS C. Yes ; I thought *you* would ask me.

DEX. (*passionately*). Mary ! (*checking himself*) I beg your pardon. (*ceremoniously*) Miss Colepepper. May I offer you my arm to the saloon ?

[*They go off arm-in-arm,* L. C.

CLAVER. (*looking up from skylight down which he has been talking*). Holloa! she's taken that fellow's arm ! Confound his impudence ! I'll teach him. (*going violently after him*) No, (*stops*) curse him ! he knows too much.

[*Exit, sulkily,* R.

Enter MOLESKIN *and* LOVIBOND, L. C., *he wears a great coat, with the collar up, and handcuffs under the long sleeves of his coat, and a large hat nearly concealing his features.*

MOLE. (L.). There's a style of toggery for the tropics ! Why, it's enough to make a man prespire to look at you. How can you ?

LOV. (R.). It's not for warmth—quite the contrary. I'm running away under 'em ! It's the natural desire of a man in my degrading position to escape observation. You *will* cruelly force me on deck, but I hope you won't compel me to show my face. They allow masks even to the prisoners at Pentonville.

MOLE. Degraded be blowed ! You're not the first nor the last gent that's had a misfortune. Besides, nobody knows but *you're* a gentleman, and *I'm* a gentleman.

LOV. But you never leave me !

MOLE. What o' that ! It's only a case o' two gentlemen that's werry fond o' one another.

LOV. And these fetters ! (*holds up his wrists to show the handcuffs.*)

MOLE. The darbies ! Oh ! keep your cuffs well down and nobody will be any the wiser.

LOV. But suppose my nose should itch, and I want to scratch it ?

MOLE. Well, in that case, you must *rub* it against something.

LOV. I suppose it's no use asserting my innocence any more ?

MOLE. Not a bit of it.

LOV. Still there's a melancholy satisfaction in repeating that I'm not the felon Downy—that I was left at Aden by the breaking down of the last P. and O. boat, in which I ought to have reached Suez. I found a dozen names before mine on the list for the Simoon, and was fool enough to jump at a berth offered me by the felon Downy, for a slight advance, little dreaming what would be the consequence.

MOLE. That's a werry feasible story, but it won't wash.

LOV. What do you mean by " it won't wash ?" (*disgusted.*)

LOV. Why should you ha' come aboard by the name of Downy, if you are somebody else ?

LOV. Because, Mr. Moleskin, at the intermediate stations, passengers are booked contingent on vacancies. Now, Downy stood No. 1 for Suez: I stood No. 10. By assuming the name of Downy I stepped into his shoes as No. 1.

MOLE. Werry artful, indeed! But how do you account for your possession of that there bag?

Lov. The felon Downy begged me to take it for him. I was to leave it at Shepherd's Hotel, Cairo. What a damned fool you are!

MOLE. (*admiringly*). Well, that's more than I can say of you. You *are* a cute 'un, Mr. Downy! But it won't do, bless you; the likelier it looks, the less I believes it. You've got no witnesses, you see, to identify you as somebody else.

Lov. (*aside*). Identify me, eh? Good heavens! Clarinda could do it at once! But then I should only get rid of the handcuffs of justice, to put on those of matrimony. Still there's no other way of redeeming my character, so here goes. Mr. Moleskin, you place me in a painful dilemma. There *is* a lady on board who can prove I'm not the felon Downy. But I must request a private interview with her, or the consequences may be awful.

MOLE. Who is it?

Lov. Mrs. Lovibond.

MOLE. I know: the fine woman with the light 'air and blue eyes. Quite the lady, *she* is. I think I might trust you with her: in course, keeping a heye on you both.

Lov. (*wiping his nose on* MOLESKIN'S *shoulder*). He told me to rub it on *something!* Hem! Then let Mrs. Lovibond know that a gentleman wishes to speak with her privately, on most particular business.

MOLE. But I must give her some name. Suppose I say "Downy?"

Lov. Call me what you will. In my position, one name's as bad as another. (*crosses to* L.)

MOLE. (*goes to skylight*). Steward! Tell Mrs. Lovibond to step upon deck, Mr. Downy wants her. You didn't think I was agoing to lose sight of you, did you, Mr. Downy? Just come back.

Lov. Yes; it's the last desperate alternative. Some people might say that it's "out of the frying pan into the fire." But on the whole I would rather endure penal servitude as Lovibond the married man, than as the felon Downy. Both sentences would be for life; but the one will be a case of convict allowance, Carpentaria, and gray and yellow dittoes. Besides, it's possible Clarinda may be changed. She may be affected by my position—this wasted form—these fettered limbs—this disgustingly familiar detective.

Enter MRS. LOVIBOND, L.

Oh! how I hate that fellow!

MRS. L. Mr. Downy seeking an interview; no doubt to apologize for his intrusion.

MAJOR McTURK *shows his head cautiously from behind the companion hatch.*

McT. A request for a private interview with Clarinda. She little thought I overheard the message. From this shelter I can watch what passes.

MOLESKIN *watches the interview from one of the gangway seats near top of skylight.*

MRS. L. Mr. Downy, you have sought an interview. I can readily guess the motive of your request. It is granted already.

Lov. (*aside*). I'll break myself to her by gentle degrees, and alter my voice a little. Madam, (*disguising his voice*) it's now some ten years ago since your husband, Augustus Lovibond——

Mrs. L. Good heavens! Mr. Downy!

Lov. Left his home in Bernard street, Russell square, at his usual hour after breakfast, on the morning of the 10th of August.

Mrs. L. Yes; from that moment I have had no tidings of him but one letter, from which——

Lov. You inferred that he had sought in another existence that repose denied him here.

Mrs. L. Oh, sir, how *do* you know this?

Lov. From the unhappy Lovibond in person.

Mrs. L. Then he didn't make away with himself?

Lov. He tried to do it, but couldn't; the man was very miserable.

Mrs. L. Alas, sir, by my fault, I'm afraid.

Lov. (*aside*). She owns it!

Mrs. L. I thought I had driven him to an untimely end.

Lov. You drove him as far in that direction as he was capable of going. But when it came to the point, he determined to live on.

Mrs L. Oh, sir, you've taken a load off my mind.

Lov. He engaged a passage to Alexandria, and thence to Singapore; and there, in honest industry, strove to forget the wife whose jealousy and too great desire for sway had driven him into exile.

Mrs. L. And he still lives, sir?

Lov. He does; in hopes of one day hearing that his wife, whom he always loved, even while he trembled under her frown, had become a changed being.

Mrs. L. Oh, sir, she has; believe me, she has. Are you in communication with him?

Lov. Yes, I see him every day. He has left Singapore. Suppose I told you he was awaiting the arrival of this vessel at Suez?

Mrs. L. I should be so happy.

Lov. It wouldn't be too much for you?

Mrs. L. No!

Lov. Suppose I told you he was on board?

Mrs. L. Oh! gracious!

Lov. That he stood before you. Here! (*strikes an attitude, removes his hat, and resumes his natural voice*) Yes, Clarinda! Behold your long-lost Gussy!

Mrs. L. Augustus! Is it possible! You stand apart. Won't you take me to your arms?

Lov. Would if I could. (*shows handcuffs*. MᶜTᴜʀᴋ *testifies by gestures his rage at the sight of the kiss, and disappears*) But I can't. These manacles! Overpowered as I am by emotion, I can't even blow my——Would you blow it for me? (*she wipes his nose with her pocket handkerchief*)

Mrs. L. A prisoner! Why, what have you done?

Lov. Nothing; but it seems Downy has done all sorts of thing. He gave me up his berth and the use of his name. No doubt he knew he was tracked, and that the officers were on board. I've been arrested for him I've sent for you to identify me. Yonder sits the detective. Speak the word, and your Augustus once more walks abroad in the proud consciousness of freedom, and a light coat better suited to the climate.

Mrs. L. I won't loose a moment! (*she goes up,* R., *to* Mᴏʟᴇsᴋɪɴ, *and speaks with him earnestly.*)

Enter Sɪʀ Sᴏʟᴏᴍᴏɴ *from companion,* L.

Sɪʀ S. Mr. Downy, allow me to present my card. (*gives card.* Lᴏᴠɪʙᴏɴᴅ *takes it awkwardly, owing to his handcuffs*) As a diplomatist, it is my peculiar function to prevent fighting. But, as a gentleman, of course, I can't refuse to be the bearer of a hostile message.

Lov. A hostile message to me! Why, I've offended nobody! (*aside*) Oh. I suppose it's meant for Downy.

Sir S. Pardon me. I am instructed to say that you have insulted a lady, to whom Major McTurk stands in the most delicate relation.

Lov. I know nothing of McTurk, or his delicate relations! I've insulted nobody.

Sir S. Pardon me. I am instructed to say that you have most grossly insulted Mrs. Lovibond : first, by entering her cabin this morning ; and, just now, by openly kissing her on deck before several witnesses.

Lov. But, suppose I'm ready to explain ?

Sir S. Pardon me ; I am instructed to say no explanation can be accepted. You will be good enough to refer me to a friend.

Lov. Sir, I have no friends ; and, if I had, I wouldn't refer you to one. But surely, as a rational man, when I tell you that Mrs. Lovibond is *my* wife——

Sir S. Your wife——

Lov. Yes, sir, my wife!

Sir S. That case was certainly not provided for in my instructions.

Lov. Perhaps you'll have the kindness to inform Major McTurk of the fact ; such will be confirmed by the lady, if referred to. (*goes up* L. *of skylight, to* Mrs. Lovibond *and* Moleskin.)

Sir S. Let me see. Here I am, thrown suddenly on my own responsibility. I was charged to insist on an appointment to fight at Suez ; but this relation between the parties alters the aspect of the negotiation. A man has, certainly, the right to enter his wife's cabin, and even kiss her before witnesses, though such conjugal endearments are in bad taste. Having, as it were, left Mr. Downy a copy of my dispatches, I think I may, with propriety, convey his explanation to the Major. . [*Exit*, L.

Lovibond, Mrs. Lovibond, *and* Moleskin *come down.*

Mole. Werry well. You say, ma'am, and will stake your davy, if necessary, that the prisoner is Augustus Lovibond—*your* husband—who left you ten years ago ?

Mrs. L. Yes.

Lov. There, sir! Remove these degrading fetters. (*holds out his wrists.*)

Mole. Stop a bit ; don't you be in an 'urry. All you say, ma'am, may be werry true ; I don't doubt it a bit. Only, you see, it proves nothing again this 'ere charge.

Lov. Why, it proves I'm Augustus Lovibond.

Mole Exactly.

Lov. And, therefore, I can't be Thomas Downy !

Mole Why not ? That don't follow—Thomas Downy has no end of aliases. Why, there's six on the warrant. How do I know Lovibond mayn't be another alias of Downy—or Downy an alias of Lovibond ?

Mrs. L. Oh, dear ! that never occurred to me ! (Lovibond *groans.*)

Mole. Besides, you've been ten years away from your good lady here. How does she know what games you may have been up to all that time ?

Lov. (*looking at* Mrs. Lovibond). Never ! never ! I've been up to nothing !

Mole. No, no, ma'am ; I'm werry sorry for your feelings—but it wont wash !

Lov. My dear, sir, what *will* wash ?

Mrs. L. What *is* to be done ? Oh, I know ; I'll consult Mr. Dexter.

He's everybody's friend. Good-bye, Augustus—keep up your spirits till I return. (*embraces him, sobbing*) Oh, dear, oh dear!

Lov. (*unable to wipe his eyes*). Clarinda, dear, do my nose again. (*she wipes his eyes, and exits,* L.) Here's a state of things! I've discovered myself to my wife, and I haven't got rid of my handcuffs!

Enter Sir Solomon, L.

Sir S. Mr. Downy, I have conveyed your explanation to my principal, Major McTurk.

Lov. Ah! of course, he's satisfied?

Sir S. Pardon me. He says that supposing you to be the husband of Mrs. Lovibond, your heartless behavior to that lady, of which she has long ago informed him, renders it more than ever his duty to call you out. It may be as well you should know he is a dead shot, and that he labors under the impression that, in shooting you he will be ridding the world of a monster.

Lov. Don't talk in that ridiculous manner! Do I look like a monster?

Sir S. You will excuse my entering upon that question. May I request that you will refer me to a friend to arrange the preliminaries.

Lov. There's the doctor. He's everybody's friend. Perhaps he won't object as mine.

Sir S. I shall take an early opportunity of conferring with him. Sir, I have the honor to wish you a very good evening.   [*Exit.* L.

Lov. Good evening! I thought Mrs. Lovibond would smooth everything. But she makes everything worse and worse! Here I am with a wife—a duel—and the handcuffs—all on my hands at once. (*down* L.)

Dex. (*down* R.). Now, my dear sir, don't give way to despair. You're safe to be identified sooner or later.

Lov. Later, I'm afraid!

Dex. The awkward part of the business is, that you've been at Singapore all the time covered by this swindler's transactions. I'm afraid the only way will be to move a postponement of your trial at the Old Bailey, 'till we can get witnesses over from the Straits, to swear you're *not* Downy.

Lov. But my arrest isn't all, doctor. I've got into a fresh scrape since Clarinda left me. Sir Solomon Fraser has brought me a challenge from Major McTurk.

Dex. A challenge! What for?

Lov. My conduct to my wife, he says——

Dex. Let me see. Yes, I think I can get you out of *that* mess.

Lov. Can you? Oh, my dear doctor——

Dex. Certainly. We'll tell the major you're in custody on a charge of felony. Of course, a man in that ignominious position forfeits all the privileges of a gentleman—including that of being popped off with a hair trigger.

Lascars *enter with lamps from companion,* R. *and* L.—*hang lamps—passen-gers* R. *and* L.,—*band* L.—*when band is on,* Lascars *exit by companion,* R. *and* L.

Lov. But the loss of my character?

Dex. Will be the saving of your life. Choose between 'em. (*a pause;* Moleskin *comes down* R.)

Lov. Go and blast my reputation. (*exit* Dexter R.) My (*passengers begin to appear on deck*) wife found! My life in danger! My reputation blighted!

MOLE. Here's the company coming up from supper. Now, Mr. Downy, (*taps him on the shoulder*) I think it's about time to turn in.

LOV. And a detective continually at my side! But let me hide my misery in my cabin. Lead on, myrmidon of the law.

. MOLE. Myr—midden! Come, Mr. Downy, I've behaved quite the gentleman to you, sir, and I didn't ought to be called out of my name —and by such a hepithet too—" Midden," indeed, Mr. Downy, I blush for you!

- LOV. That's the climax! *He* blushes for me! (*they go up* R., *as* LOVIBOND *approaches the companion*, DEXTER *enters*, R.) Well, doctor, you've seen the major's friend?

DEX. I've seen the major.

LOV. And, of course the challenge is off?

DEX. On the contrary; he says he'll wait the result of your trial. If you're found guilty, he will leave you to the law. But if you're acquitted, he'll call you out the day after.

LOV. Good heavens! I said the climax was attained. This caps the climax! [*Exeunt* LOVIBOND *and* MOLESKIN, R.

SMART, R., *and* HARDISTY, L , *come down. Enter* MRS. SEBRIGHT, COLE-PEPPER, MRS. LOVIBOND, SIR SOLOMON, MISS COLEPEPPER, CLAV-ERING, MRS. RABBITS, *and other passengers, and* McTURK ; *group at top.*

DEX. (*to* SMART). Captain, with your permission, the passengers propose a dance on deck.

SMART. All right, Doctor. (DEXTER *goes up*) I'm going to turn in, Hardisty. You'll see the look-outs relieved. It's a fine night, but the moon will bring up a haze with it, and we're not far from the Mazaffa Reefs.

HARD. Aye, aye, sir. [*Exit* SMART, R.

MRS. S. (*coming down to* DEXTER). Oh, doctor! both Sir Solomon and Mr. Colepepper want to dance with me. If I accept either, I know the other will be so angry; so I told both I was engaged to *you*.

DEX. Really, as John Sebright's friend, I don't like this lavish resort to fibbing.

MRS. S. Please don't say fibbing

DEX. Taradiddles, at all events. I've a good mind to throw you over.

MRS. S. Oh, please, doctor, if you'll look over it, only this one.

DEX. Well, as there's no great harm done, and as you are certainly the prettiest partner on board—come along.

A dance is formed: SIR SOLOMON *and* MRS. RABBITS ; COLEPEPPER *and* MRS. LOVIBOND : CLAVERING *and* MISS COLEPEPPER ; DEXTER *and* MRS. SEBRIGHT ; *and passengers. In the middle of dance, i. e., after galop, cry from the fore part of the ship—"Breakers ahead on the port bow." Tremendous crash, which sends all the passengers reeling.*

HARD. (*seizing his trumpet at rail*). Hard a-port—hard all—(*to* DEXTER) By heavens, doctor, she's ashore on the Mazaffa Reef!

DEX. Call the captain. I'll keep order here. (*another heavy sound is heard, and steam being let off.*)

HARD. (*through the trumpet*). Below there! Reverse!

DEX. (*snatching trumpet from him*). Go ahead—full steam! (*to engine-room. To* HARDISTY) If we back her, she may go down in deep water. (*the ladies scream violently—all this passes very rapidly.*)

McT. } Lower the boats!
Cole. } Mary! keep close to me! (*children scream from below the sky-light—confusion on board—women run about in terror.*)
Dex. (*very loud*). Silence, all, for your lives! (*a sudden pause*) Be cool and obey orders, and all shall be safe on shore in an hour's time.

Enter Smart, r. c.

Smart. Thank you for that, doctor! (*through the trumpet*) Pipe han'ds to boat stations! (*boatswain's whistle heard*) Boat's crews stand by the tackle falls. (*they do so*) Lower away and keep off! Carpenter's mates, stand by to cut away masts! (*Chinamen do so.*)
Hard. (*coming up to* Smart). She's heeling over fast. The starboard cabins are filling! The doors are jammed! The women and children will be drowned!
Dex. We must jump down and pass 'em up by the skylight! Here goes to save the women and children! (*throws his coat off—jumps down into the skylight and passes up children.*)
Hard. Heads below! (*follows* Dexter.)
Miss C. Papa! papa!
Mrs. S. (*in terror*). Mr. Colepepper! Sir Solomon! Oh, dear, will nobody save me?
Mrs. L. (*to* McTurk). Hector! (*tries to cling to him.*)
McT. (*shaking both off*). Hands off! £50 for a place in the first boat!

Enter Lovibond *and* Moleskin, l. c.—*they cross to* r.—Lovibond *sinks on the stage, flat on his back.*

Mrs. L. Augustus! you'll save me? (*crosses to him.*)
Lov. I can't swim in handcuffs!

Tableau.

ACT III.

Scene.—*A coral reef coming down to the edge of the sea, which is seen in flat.* Tottle *discovered on guard over the stores, armed with a musket and cutlass—*Hardisty *sitting on a case, making entries in pencil in a book.*

Dex. (*calling from within the tent*). Four dozen soup and bouilli!
Hard. (*writing in his book*). Forty-eight S. and B.
Dex. Three dozen roast beef.
Hard. Thirty-six R. B.
Dex. Two dozen and a half pheasants.
Hard. Thirty pheas.
Dex. Four dozen gelatine.
Hard Forty-eight gal.
Dex. That finishes the preserved meats; and now belay, Hardisty, till I calculate the distribution to the messes.
Hard. (*putting away his book*). Well, we shan't starve yet a while, that's a comfort. (*comes down,* l.)

Enter Capt. Smart—*his arm in a sling*—1 e. r.

Smart. Well, Hardisty ?

Hard. On your pins again, captain ?

Smart. Yes ; Dexter has patched me up. I thought it was all over with me, when that spar knocked me out of the chains. Well, Tottle ?

Tot. I'm on duty, captain—standing sentry over the stores—or I'd have made bold to ask for a grip of your fist, though it's clean agin discipline, I know.

Smart. Thanks, my good fellow. I'm glad to see everything looking so ship-shape.

Hard. Ah ! we may thank Dexter for that. You may imagine the state of things on board after you were disabled.

Smart. That I can—what, with lubberly Lascars, useless invalids, frightened women, and squalling babies.

Hard. Officers and quartermasters did their duty like Englishmen— the passengers behaved well on the whole—but Dexter was our life and soul. She struck at nine, and, thanks to him, we had every man, wo- man, and child ashore, tents rigged, passengers under cover, and all with a comfortable basin of soup in either hold by six in the morning.

Tot. And that ain't half, captain. Why, he's collected the stores, settled the messes, regulated the allowances, parcelled out the duty. Blest if he ain't been steward, cook, and bottle-washer, to say nothing of purser, doctor, and loblolly boy. I never see such a beggar to turn his hand to things ! (*goes up with* Hardisty.)

Enter Dexter *from the tent,* l. u. e. .

Dex. Belay there, Tottle ! or if you *will* sing my praises, sing 'em smaller. Well, Captain, 1 said, I should have you afloat again in three days, and here you are.

Smart. Timbers a little battered ; but good for Lloyd's A. 1. list for many a year to come. (*shakes hands with him*) Dexter, I owe you a life.

Dex. Be as long as possible in paying me, then. I hope you approve of our arrangements ?

Smart. Couldn't be better. I say, how about provisions ?

Dex. We've enough for a fortnight, at least, with care.

Smart. And drinkables ?

Dex. Ah ! we might be better off there. About forty dozen of beer, half as much claret——

Smart. But water ?

Dex. Only two hogsheads. The first nearly expended in the three days we've been here—I mean to keep the last for the children and the sick.

Smart. God help us all, if drink runs short !

Dex. Oh, never fear. I think I could manage to rig up a distilling apparatus out of the ship's coppers and a few musket barrels. Besides, after consultation with Hardisty, I've sent off the second officer with the pinnance, to cruise about the Straits, in hopes they may pick up a steamer and send her to our relief.

Smart. The best thing you have done yet—and everything you've done is good. By George ! Dexter, I feel ashamed to take the command out of your hand.

Dex. I don't mean you to—for a week yet, at least. I shall have you on your beam-ends again, if you go fagging about too soon. So be a good child, and go back to bye-bye.

Smart. Not I ; I'm quite fit for duty, I tell you.

DEX. I know better. What! you won't go quietly? Here, Harαisty. (HARDISTY *comes down*, R. H.) Carry this naughty baby to bed.

HARD. Come, Captain.

SMART. I suppose I must obey orders. God bless you, my fine fellow! If prayers go the right road, *you* ought to be all safe up there. (*pointing to heaven.*)   [*Exit*, R. H., *leaning on* HARDISTY.

DEX. There's no prayer like work, depend upon it, Captain.

Enter COLEPEPPER, L.

COLE. My own theory, Doctor. But you illustrate it by practice. Here's my report of the stores washed up from the wreck this last tide. (*gives paper.*)

DEX. (*taking paper and glancing at it*). One of the tanks of ice, I see. Just the thing for my *coup-de-soleil* patients.

COLE. What a mercy it is we've so few sick. For my own part, I haven't felt half so well for the last twenty years.

DEX. Because you've never thought half so little of yourself, or half so much of other people. Hard work to a good purpose is the best *elixir vitæ* I know.

COLE. You're right, Mr. Dexter. Egad! I feel equal to anything. I could roll up a harness-cask—light a fire—cook a copper of soup—knock kown Sir Solomon!—Come! what have you got for me to do this morning?

DEX. There's the wood to chop for the fire; and the preserved meat tins to open for the mess rations.

COLE. Oh! that's mere laborer's work. Do you know. I think I could make a sea-pie. Do let me try my hand at a sea-pie.

DEX. No! that's high art. Your first is safe to be uneatable; and we can't afford experiments. But I applaud your ambition.

COLE. Ah! Mr. Dexter, thanks to you for it—as for so much besides. My poor Mary, but for your care that night——

DEX. (*interrupting*). Look! Here comes Sir Solomon. He doesn't thrive on difficulty, like you. You must have observed the melancholy change in him?

COLE. Melancholy change? You mean his silence? I call it the greatest change for the better I ever knew.

Enter SIR SOLOMON, 3 E. L , *down* C., *his jaws tied up with a handkerchief—a boot on one foot and a shoe on the other—and looks generally dilapidated and seedy.*

DEX. Why, Sir Solomon, (SIR SOLOMON *bows*) I hope you're not suffering from tooth-ache? (SIR SOLOMON *shakes his head ruefully, intimating that he is*) Allow me to look at the peccant grinders. (SIR SOLOMON, *with great eagerness, resists any attempt to look into his mouth.*)

COLE. Come, Sir Solomon, don't be down in the mouth. (SIR SOLOMON *makes a grimace at the word mouth*) Follow my example. Make yourself generally useful.

DEX. Come, sir, we'd better look out the meat cans for to-day's rations. (*they go up to store tent*, R. U. E.)

SIR S. (*speaking with difficulty; as he opens his mouth, an entire loss of teeth is apparent*). Tooth-ache! I wish I had! Down in the mouth! well I may be! They may have been washed ashore.

Enter LIMPET, U. E. R., *as if searching. He wears an old pair of red plush breeches.*

Found 'em, Limpet?

LIMP. (*in a mournful voice*). No, Sir Solomon, I've walked all round the reef; but there's no signs on 'em.

SIR S. Continue your search.   [*Exit* LIMPET, L., *behind tent.*

Enter MRS. SEBRIGHT, *from the women's tent,* R. *She looks gay and cheerful, and wears a coquettish made-up costume, and handkerchief tied over her head.*

MRS. S. Ah! Good morning, doctor; good morning, Mr. Colepepper. Hard at work, I see, as usual; Sir Solomon, too. (SIR SOLOMON *turns ruefully and bows*) No; he's *not* hard at work as usual. (*laughs*) Oh, dear! Oh, dear! You poor, dear, dilapidated man. Do let me take you into hospital and nurse you. What! no reply? Then you're an ungrateful monster!

SIR SOLOMON *intimates his thanks by signs, and strolls off sadly,* R. U. E., DEXTER *and* COLEPEPPER *come down* L.

MRS. S. I've developed such a talent for nursing since we were wrecked—haven't I, doctor?

DEX. That you have. Mr. Colepepper, I call this lady and your daughter my two sisters of charity. I expected a right hand in Miss Colepepper, but I confess——

MRS. S. You thought Jenny Sebright more ornamental than useful. I hope I've redeemed my character.

COLE. You've not discarded the ornamental, I'm happy to see. That dress is monstrously becoming.

MRS. S. I'm glad you like it. I contrived it last night when I was sitting up with Mrs. Rabbits' babies. Little Polly's so much better this morning, doctor.

DEX. Ah! that means that you've attended carefully to my directions through the night?

MRS. S. Oh, yes! I gave her her draught every half hour. Poor little darling! she was so thankful—and her poor sick mother, too. Oh! doctor, how shall I ever thank you enough for teaching me how much pleasanter it is to wait than to be waited upon.

COLE. What! *you've* learnt that lesson, too, my dear madam?

MRS. S. Oh! doctor, it was so pitiful to hear the little darlings cry all through the night, "Water, water!" Couldn't you allow 'em a pint a piece extra?

DEX. Impossible, I'm afraid.

MRS. S. I'll give up half mine; so will Miss Colepepper, I'm sure; and Mrs. Lovibond; and all of us.

DEX. I've no objection to that. The more you give up, the better you'll thrive on what's left. But I've work for you down at the men's hospital.

MRS. S. Oh, I'm so glad! What is it?

DEX. To attend on one of the steerage passengers. He had a *coup-de-soleil* yesterday, and is delirious this morning. I'm afraid of congestion. I want some one to keep applying ice to his head. He's an odd, mysterious fellow—and nobody seems to care much about nursing him.

MRS. S. I shall be ready directly. I'll just go and see my little charges tucked up comfortably, and show Mrs. Rabbits' Ayah how to make arrowroot properly. I say, couldn't you allow me a leetle extra claret to mix with it, doctor?

DEX. (*peremptorily*). No; I tell you!

MRS. S. (*coaxingly*). Only half a bottle ; and every drop of it for the babies, you know.

DEX. Hang the woman ! she'd wheedle a boatswain's mate ! Here, Tottle ; serve out half a bottle of claret to Mrs. Sebright.

TOT. Aye, aye, sir ! Here you are, ma'am.

MRS. S. (*aside to* TOTTLE). You can stop it off my next two days' allowance, you know, Mr. Tottle. (*she goes up to store tent,* L.)

COLE. What a transformation !

DEX. No ; what a revelation ! It was all there ; but it wanted the occasion to show itself.

COLE Why, there wasn't a lady on board took so much waiting on !

DEX. Because there wasn't a lady on board who had so much offered her. And among the civilest of her civil servants were Sir Solomon and yourself.

COLE. I'm afraid I was very near making a fool of myself. (*Exit* MRS. SEBRIGHT *into tent,* R.) But I've reflected since the wreck. Ah ! Mary.

Enter MISS COLEPEPPER, R. *She has a pretty extempore head-dress.*

MISS C. Dear papa ! (*kisses him*) Mr. Dexter—(*shakes hands with him*) how well papa's looking ; isn't he ?

DEX. And you, Miss Colepepper. Why, hardship seems to agree with your family.

MISS C. Oh ! I knew papa would come out under difficulties. He always does. Bless him ! And with your example, Mr. Dexter, we should indeed be cowards to refuse what little help we can give.

DEX. Then, sir, just show your daughter that ice they've got ashore. And you get a basket of it, (*to* MISS COLEPEPPER) and bring it to me here. I'll walk down with you and Mrs. Sebright to the hospital, and show you how to use it.

COLE. (*going up to store tent*). I'll get you a basket, my love.

MISS C. (*to* DEXTER). Oh ! I'm so thankful that this accident has shown you papa in his true colors.

DEX. Now, for the first time, I understand how you come to be father and daughter. Ah ! Miss Colepepper, this is life—stripped to the buff. In our artificial world men are so buckrammed, and padded, and corsoled by aids and appliances, that they neither show nor use their muscles. After all, we may have a few curs among us ; but, on the whole, Englishmen peel well ; don't they ?

MISS C. And Englishwomen ?

DEX. What—*you* fishing for a compliment !

COLE (*coming down with basket,* L.). Here's the basket, Mary. The ice is only a few hundred yards along the reef.

MISS C. Come along, papa. (*crosses to him*) I'll be with you again directly, Mr. Dexter. [*Exeunt* MR. *and* MISS COLEPEPPER, 1 E. L.

DEX. Oh ! what a wife that girl would make ! It's enough to drive a fellow wild to think of her being wasted on a loose, idle, pleasure-loving gambler like Clavering ; and all because he's well-born, good-looking, and has heavy interest to back him ! But to think of old Colepepper turning up such a trump ! He can't know this Clavering's real character, or he'd never——But Mary don't care a fig for him—that's a comfort ! I've an enormous faith in women's wits and wills.

Enter MRS. SEBRIGHT, *from tent,* R.

MRS. S. Thank you for the compliment. You so seldom pay one.

DEX. And that wasn't meant for *you*. But, come ; don't look vexed.

I shall have a better account of you to give to Jack than I dared have hoped a week ago. Miss Colepepper is to walk down with us. She's gone for the ice with her old trump of a father. I say, how he *has* improved.

MRS. S. In all ways. Amongst others, he hasn't said a tender word to *me* since we were wrecked. I suppose he's too busy—but it's a great comfort.

DEX. And has Sir Solomon been equally sensible ?

MRS. S. Ah ! *he* hasn't said a word to anybody—I can't think what's come over him !

DEX. Let's take the good sent us, and ask no questions. Sir Solomon is what Sydney Smith called—a brilliant flash of silence.

MRS. S. At all events, I begin to hope they've both given up thinking of poor me—I can meet Jack so happily now.

DEX. Remember, you'll have to give back Sir Solomon's diamonds, and Mr. Colepepper's shawl.

MRS. S. You spiteful creature ! As if I'd had any pleasure out of 'em ! Why, you've got both. But I'm so thankful you have. I feel very good now ; but there's no saying what such temptations might do —and, you know, we may have to live here all the rest of our lives— and then there'd be no Jack in the way.

DEX. Here comes Miss Colepepper with the ice.

Enter MISS COLEPEPPER, 1 L. E.

MISS C. Now then. Ah ! Mrs. Sebright, your smiling face isn't a bit the worse for your night's nursing. Oh ! Mr. Dexter, if you'd seen her hushing those poor fretful babies !

MRS. S. Not half so fretful as their poor mother—and you know you were up half the night with her.

DEX. Come, I can't have any quarrelling over your respective good works. Hospital mates ! right face ; quick march ! (*takes them both on his arm, and exits,* 1 R. E.)

Enter LIMPET, 1 L. E.

LIMP. Not a trace of 'em ! Sir Solomon's teeth have been swallowed up in the jaws of the hocean ! Well, I hope they look better in the hocean's jaws, than they did in Sir Solomon's. I little thought, when my guv'nor came down by the run into the boat that night, that he'd knocked the whole set out of his head, as clean as a whistle. Well, it's a good job ! for he can't give so many horders as he used, nor talk such a d—d deal o' nonsense.

Enter MRS. GRIMWOOD, *disconsolately, from the tent,* R., *with a cap in her hand.*

Ah ! Mrs. Grimwood ! Good day, Mrs. Grimwood !

GRIM. Oh, Mr. Limpet ! here's a melancholy situation. I couldn't ha' believed I ever should ha' got through three days of it.

LIMP. Nor me, neither, Mrs. Grimwood. And if master had been in his usual way, why, I couldn't—I *couldn't*.

GRIM. To think of people that's been used to their comforts having to pig in tents like gipsies, or so many Robinson Crusoes.

LIMP. No conveniencies for meals, nor nothing.

GRIM. Not so much as a flat-iron, if I wanted to get up any little fine thing for myself, or my young lady. Here's a cap—rough-drying is the hutmost I can manage!

LIMP. Ah! when one *reads* of people being cast away on desolate hilands, one don't realize the 'ardships of it. I give you my word, I 'aven't seen a comb or brush these three days. Just look at my head. (*takes off hat.*)

GRIM. And as I was below when the vessel struck—would you believe it?—I had to come ashore without so much as a crinoline!

LIMP. Well, I shouldn't have noticed it, if you hadn't spoke about it, Mrs Grimwood.

GRIM. (*looking at his red plush breeches*). But—gracious 'evins! wot's that? (*pointing to them*) You've never gone back to livery, Mr. Limpet?

LIMP. What was a man to do? with his pantaloons a wreck, like the wessel? These disgusting things was washed on shore; and I was thankful for 'em!

GRIM. Ah!

LIMP. But my guv'nor has lost suffen what's worse nor crinolines and pantaloons, Mrs. Grimwood, I can tell you!

GRIM. What hever can *that* be, Mr. Limpet?

LIMP. Well, he's lost—his teeth!

GRIM. Real?

LIMP. No! they were not real; but mineral succeed-in-of-em!

GRIM. Gracious 'evins! Poor gentleman! Well, it ought to teach *us* submission. But—what's worse than all—to see one's missus so cheerful and heasy, and making the best of heverything to that degree—it's enough to provoke a saint!

LIMP. Ah! Sir Solomon don't take that line, I can tell you.

GRIM. Would you believe it? she actually demeans herself to wait upon the men in the hospital. Not gentlefolks, you know; but common sailors and soldiers—and such like.

LIMP. Ah! misery—they say—makes a man acquainted with strange bed-fellows!

GRIM. (*offended*). Really, Mr. Limpet!

LIMP. Meaning, no offence, Mrs. Grimwood!

GRIM. Which if one is cast on a desolate hiland, and without the common necessaries of life, one at least expects the respect due to a female! Bedfellows, indeed! Bedfellows! well, I'm sure!

Exit into tent R., *offended.*

LIMP. She hevidedtly turned up her nose. Well, there's such a thing as being *nasty* particular. Oh! here comes Sir Solomon. I wonder if he's found his teeth? He mustn't catch me a philandering with the females, and so I'll hook it. [*Exit*, 1 E. L.

Enter SIR SOLOMON, 1 E. R.

SIR S. Can't see 'em anywhere. I've completed the round of the reef, and all in vain! I must manage till we reach Cairo. I suppose there's a dentist there. These preserved meats are a mercy! If we had been reduced to hard locusts and junk, I should have starved! I've lost everything, even my umbrella—and walking under the sun is highly dangerous to the brain. If I could provide some substitute. Ha! (*finds a hamper lid*) This, I think, with a little ingenuity, and a piece of ropeyarn—(*adjusts the hamper lid on his head, like a mushroom hat*) Let me resume my search. [*Exit*, R. U. E.

Enter MAJOR McTURK, 1 E. L. *He looks abject and dishevelled, and limps.*

McT. This infernai corai cuts like a razor, and I escaped in my dress boots. What with the sun overhead and the reef under foot—and only half enough to eat, and not near half enough to drink—I feel so low and poorly. (*sits on a box, disconsolately*) I'd hang myself, only there isn't a tree on the reef to fasten a rope to. What's half a bottle of beer for a fellow ? I can't bear it much longer. And such a lot stored away, yonder. I dare say Dexter helps himself, eh ? There's only the sentry. Here ! sentry, I say ; I want to speak to you !

Tot. (*coming forward, c.*). Aye, aye, sir !

McT. I'm very bad, sentry !

Tot. Which my name's Tottle, sir. I ain't a soger, sir, I'm a steward.

McT. Yes, Mr. Tottle, I remember. I'm dying for a drop of beer, or wine, or brandy—anything strong. There's lots in store ; nobody would know if we helped ourselves to a bottle apiece. (Tottle *is silent*) Perhaps you don't want one. In that case, suppose you let me have both. I'd give you a five pound note—ten—twenty ! Say how much ?

Tot. You white-livered son of a sea-cook ! Why, the very women ought to be let loose upon you, to scratch your eyes out ! You a man !

McT. (*abjectly*). Oh ! don't be angry, Mr. Tottle ; and don't speak so loud ! I wasn't in earnest ; I wasn't indeed ! I only wanted to try you.

Tot. To *try* me ! If you don't deserve six dozen at the gangway, without trial, may I never crack another biscuit ! You mean. paltry——

McT. Oh ! Mr. Tottle, somebody will hear you !

Tot. I wish every soul on the reef could hear me. Be off ! you poor, selfish, sniveling hound ! Be off ! or I'll drive my bayonet through your dirty carcass !

McT. Oh, dear ! oh, dear ! What shall I do ?

Tot. Be off, I say !

McT. I'm going, Mr. Tottle ! [*Exit* McTurk, 1 L. E.

Tot. And that's the chap that used to talk blood and thunder at the saloon table till you'd shake in your shoes to hear him. I suppose delirium trimmings will be the end o' him.

Lov. (*singing without*).
　A light heart and a good pair of top boots
　　Will go through the world, my brave boys.

Tot. Why, if it ain't that 'ere Downy. Well, he thrives on half-allowance, *surely.*

Enter Lovibond, 1 R. E.

Lov. Ah, Tottle, my boy ! how d'ye do ?

Tot. Hearty, thank you, sir ! how are you ?

Lov. That's your sort. I'm charming ; and the air of this watering-place makes me feel that it must be near breakfast time.

Tot. Glad to see you've got your eatin' tackle aboard again, sir.

Lov. Yes, Tottle, such delightful weather ; and such a nice open situation as this is for enjoying the weather.

Tot And how's that werry partic'lar friend o' yourn, sir ?

Lov. Moleskin, eh ? Oh, *he's* all right. Came ashore in his slippers —cut his feet all to pieces on the reef—can't walk a step, I'm happy to say. That's why he isn't with me, as usual ! I've got a capital pair of boots, you see. He wanted me to share 'em with him, but I declined— a pair of boots are like man and wife—they ought never to be divided. (Tottle *goes up*, L., *laughing*) And talking of man and wife, where's mine, I wonder ? I told her I should pay her a visit this morning. Hoy, Clarinda !

Enter Mrs. Lovibond, *from tent*, R.

Mrs L. Here, Augustus, dear——

Lov. "Here, Augustus, dear!" but you weren't *here*. I particularly told you to be waiting for me, and when I tell you a thing, I mean you to do it, my dear.

Mrs. L. I'm very sorry, dear. I was all ready, but I'd some poor creatures to attend to in the tent.

Lov. You had one poor creature to attend to *out* of the tent, and that is your Augustus !

Mrs. L. I'll be careful not to keep you waiting another time, dear.

Lov. Oh, I'm not angry, Clarinda ; I'm too happy to be angry ! Only think, that poor devil, Moleskin, limped dreadfully yesterday. But he can't stir a peg to-day, without my boots ; and, of course, I know better than to lend him them.

Mrs. L. Oh, I'm so glad to see he's taken off the handcuffs !

Lov. He couldn't help himself. 1 declared if he didn't take 'em off, I wouldn't fetch him his rations. In short, my dear, for to-day, at least, I'm master of the situation.

Mrs. L. How delightful ! We can have such a nice ramble about the reef together. I've so much to tell you—ten years arrears, you know, to make up.

Lov. You won't be jealous ?

Mrs. L. No, dear ; I hope I've got over that folly.

Lov. When I first made myself known to you, I craned at it tremendously.

Mrs. L. Craned, dear.

Lov. Yes, I was frightened, my love. But now I'm satisfied it was the best day's work I ever did in my life. You don't bully, and you ain't jealous. You always were a duck of a lady, if it hadn't been for your little peculiarities in that way—and now—by Jove, Clarinda, you're perfection !

Mrs. L. Oh, Augustus, how happy you make me by saying that ! So long as you continue of that way of thinking, I never can be jealous !

Lov. And so long as you're not jealous, I shall continue of that way of thinking. Yes, Clarinda, I've made a very pretty little fortune in Singapore. And how we *will* enjoy it together ! I've sowed my wild oats !

Mrs. L. Augustus, love !

Lov. Mine have been a very mild crop, I can assure you.

Mrs. L. And mine have never been sowed at all !

Lov. Then I value you all the more for it. If you've been faithful to the memory of your Augustus, what will you be to the amiable reality ? I see before us a long vista of matrimonial felicity, dotted, at intervals, with little Lovibonds. But, oh, gracious ! (*suddenly crestfallen*) I'm forgetting the felon, Downy, all this time—my infernal alias—who knows if the rest of my existence mayn't be dragged out in a penal settlement ?

Mrs. L. Oh, surely you must be able to prove an alibi ?

Lov. I don't see my way to it. I've heard the strong points of the case against me put forward so continually for the last three days by the indefatigable Moleskin, that I begin to believe I'm safe to be convicted by any intelligent jury of my countrymen.

Mrs. L. Let's hope you won't have an intelligent jury, dear.

Lov. I think that highly probable. Now, leave me to steel my mind for the worst ! So, kiss me quick and go, my honey.

Mrs. L. I'll do anything you bid me, dear. Good-by till you see me again. [*Exit*, R. *tent.*

Lov. Now, I call that a woman ; and since she's so changed—she's an angel—better than an angel ! She hasn't any wings to fly away with ;

and she *has* something to sit down upon! But, no; let me not indulge in idle levity. Let me call up mental pictures of myself as a convict, or as a bleeding victim under the bullet of Major McTurk. (*goes towards the sea*) Let me wander by the sad sea wave, and contemplate. There lies our noble vessel, all on one side, like an ill-roasted egg. What's that, I wonder, glittering on the sand? Snuff-box, I hope; soap-dish, I fear; (*picks up* SIR SOLOMON's *set of teeth*) teeth, by jingo! Now, somebody must be uncommonly inconvenienced by the loss of them. I'll be magnanimous—I'll advertise 'em. No; I won't do that, because we're very short of provisions. Yes, I will. Here, Tottle, a pen, ink, and paper.

TOT. Aye; aye, sir! (*gets them, and puts them on box,* L.)

LOV. (*writes*). Lost—no! Found, a set of artificial teeth. They may be had by the owner applying to Augustus Lovibond. Confound it, though! I'm known among the passengers in general as Downy. I suppose I must sign that hated name. There! (*fixes the paper on the spar, by the side of the gong*) And now to chew the bitter cud of fancy till breakfast time. [*Exit,* 1 E. R.

Enter COLEPEPPER, 1 E. L.

COLE. So, that's off my mind. I've told Clavering the difficulty about my accounts—and he cries off! All the better. How shall I break it to poor Mary, though? She used to fancy this Clavering a hero. I'm glad, too, that I've had the wisdom to break off with the pretty widow. What would she have thought if she had found herself married to some eight lacs of debt to Government? And the poor little thing liked me —that was clear. But those *infernal vouchers!* No! as a man it is my duty to give up all idea of the widow.

Enter MISS COLEPEPPER, 1 E. R.

MISS C. Ah, papa, dear, I met Captain Clavering as I came along, looking so blank and gloomy. He merely bowed to me as he passed.

COLE. My darling are you brave enough to bear a great shock?

MISS C. Any shock *you* can give me, I'm sure.

COLE. Captain Clavering has proposed for you.

MISS C. Oh, papa!

COLE. As a man of honor, I felt it my duty to tell him the position of my unsettled accounts.

MISS C. I know—those vouchers.

COLE. I offered him an opportunity of renewing his offer.

MISS C. (*eagerly*). And he——

COLE. Nerve yourself, darling——

MISS C. I am nerved, sir. Oh, speak! He renewed it?

COLE. No; he declined.

MISS C. Thank heaven! (*drawing a deep breath as if relieved.*)

COLE. What! you are not distressed to hear it?

MISS C. Oh, you have taken such a load off my mind! I dreaded that offer—I feared you would favor Captain Clavering's suit. I once thought him all a man should be. You watched our intimacy while I lived in that delusion—I have learned better now.

COLE. My dear girl! you've taken a load off *my* heart! With what a light heart I shall go to chop the wood to boil the soup! [*Exit,* 1 E. L.

MISS C. Free at last! Free to let my heart follow the path it has been struggling so hard to take, yet dare not! He is here!

Enter DEXTER, 1 E. R.

Dex. I've come to tell you it's nearly time for you to release Mrs. Sebright. She has been managing her rebellious subject capitally. Don't be frightened at his ravings. For a delirious patient, or a kicking horse, there's nothing like a lady's hand.

Miss C. Oh, I feel happy enough this morning to face a whole legion of lunatics!

Dex. Indeed! you do look radiant!

Miss C. If you knew what good reasons I have. But are you not my best friend? Ought you not to know my happiness?

Dex. That's for you to answer—not me.

Miss C. Yes; you shall know it. Captain Clavering has withdrawn his pretensions to my hand.

Dex. I'm glad to hear it—for your sake! He's a gambler—and all gamblers are mean, selfish, and unprincipled.

Miss C. His conduct proves you have measured him right. He withdrew because papa told him of the Government claims against him, on account of the vouchers he lost in the mutiny.

Dex. The vouchers! Then Sir Solomon's story was *not* a calumny. I really beg his pardon. But about these vouchers? If recovered, they would set your father straight with the Government?

Miss C. Yes.

Dex. See, Miss Colepepper, what comes of people standing too much on their dignity! When I called on your father in Calcutta, it was mainly that I might restore to him a box of papers, which I had recovered from the mutineers, and which I believe to have contained the very vouchers—the want of which may ruin him.

Miss C. Is it possible? But where is that box now?

Dex. Under twenty fathoms of Red Sea water, and the stevedores only know how many tons of luggage. It went down aboard the Simoon.

Miss C. Oh, hard chance. But we must face our fate without them. It will not be a harder one than I can bear. I am sure you have seen both papa and I can encounter hardship. (*crosses*, R.) But I'm forgetting poor Mrs. Sebright. Good-bye! Think of me as a free and happy woman.   [*Exit*, 1 E. R.

Dex. Tottle! You remember a black box of mine?

Tot. Yes, sir. I thought to myself—when I see you with that and a carpet-bag—well, that's the lightest lot of luggage ever came aboard a P. and O. boat, homeward bound.

Dex. Do you remember where it was stowed?

Tot. In the after-hold, sir.

Dex. What water's over that part of her, do you think?

Tot. About ten fathom, sir.

Dex. All right. Look me out a dry suit of clothes, and bring them down to the beach when I hail. If anybody asks for me, say I shall be back soon. If perseverance and headers can do it, I *may* bring up those vouchers yet.   [*Exit*, L. U. E.

Enter MRS. SEBRIGHT, R.

Mrs. S. Tottle, where's the doctor?

Tot. Gone, ma'am. He'll be back soon.

Mrs. S. I want to report my patient.

Enter LOVIBOND *in reflection*, 1 E. R.

Mr. Lovibond. (*faces him and addresses him sharply*) stand and deliver!

Lov. Good gracious, Mrs Sebright, I was ruminating.

Mrs. S. What a very vaccine occupation! But I'm very angry with you. You never came to the hospital, as you promised. I've had so much on these poor unassisted little hands.

Lov. (*kissing them*). Let me add the weight of that to their burdens.

Mrs. S. You mustn't.

Lov. Oh, yes I may—my wife says I may—and when a man's wife says he may—he may.

Mrs. S. You wouldn't think, to look at them, that they had been holding down a raving maniac! Such a strong man, too!

Lov. I should think you likelier to make madmen, than to manage them!

Mrs. S. Don't talk nonsense! Only think, my patient mixed your name up in his ravings. It was all a jumble of Lovibond and Downy—and how he was Downy and you weren't, and you were—and how he'd done the detective and a black leather bag—and bills, and money hidden away on the reef—and wanting me to let him go to dig it up and hide it again.

Lov. (*through this speech has betrayed the liveliest signs of emotion*). Describe your patient.

Mrs. S. A plain man—about your size—in fact, a good deal like you altogether.

Lov. With a large scar on his right temple?

Mrs. S. Yes; do you know him?

Lov. (*sits down and begins taking off his boots*). Mrs. Sebright, I want you—I want you to put on these boots.

Mrs. S. No; I can't do that.

Lov. No; I don't mean that. May I trouble you to take these boots to Mr. Moleskin, with my compliments, and beg him to put them on, and to walk down to the hospital and listen to the ravings of your patient, and act accordingly.

Mrs. S. What do you mean?

Lov. Never *you* mind my meaning. Only carry my message. (*crosses c.,*

Mrs. S. Is *he* mad, too?

Lov. No, he isn't; but he shortly will be if you don't do what he asks you.

Mrs. S. Well, I'll go; but——

Lov. But you want to be paid for your good news, I suppose? and there! (*seizes her in his arms, and commences hugging and kissing her.*)

Enter Mrs. Lovibond, *from tent*, R.

Mrs. L. Augustus!

Lov. I'm a child of impulse, Clarinda! You're *not* jealous.

Mrs. S. No! but she has the common feelings of a woman! My dear Mrs. Lovibond. I sympathize with you.

Lov. Now, don't stop to do that. Only carry my message. Insist on his putting on the boots, whether they fit him or not. Say it's to further the ends of justice, and he'll get into 'em if he grows a crop of corns for the rest of his life. I'll have another kiss if you don't go!

Mrs. S. Mad—raving mad! another *coup-de-soleil!*

Lov. Nay, then! (*rushes at her again.*)

Mrs. S. Oh, Lord! (*screams and runs off*, 1 E. R.)

Mrs. L. (*falling on a packing-case, and sobbing hysterically*). Augustus! if you're not insane, I am the most miserable of women.

Lov. On the contrary; I am sane, and you're the happiest of your sex! She's found the real Downy!

Mrs. L. Is it possible?

Lov. He must have shipped in the steerage under one of his many aliases.

Mrs. L. But how has he betrayed himself?

Lov. He's gone beside himself; and the insane half of him has split upon the other. Well, now I am free and easy!

Mrs. L. That you certainly were, just now, with Mrs. Sebright—you were kissing her.

Lov. Was I? Well, I'll kiss you and balance the books.

Mrs. L. Let us run and tell this good news to Mr. Dexter.

Lov. By all means. (*suddenly feels the sharp coral under his feet*) O, I forgot I'd sent Moleskin my boots—I can't stir. This is the most nubbly spot in the island.

Mrs. L. Mr. Dexter must be the first to congratulate us. Now, don't you move.   [*Exit* 1 E. L.

Lov. It's all very well to say don't move, I can't. This is the most nubbly spot on the island! This blessed news has confused my naturally lucid intellect. Let me reflect! If it wasn't for that fire-eating McTurk, my horizon would be all serene! Ha! somebody coming! McTurk! Oh! heavens! Let me conceal myself. He's capable of calling me out on the spot. (*hides himself in tent,* R.)

Enter McTurk, 1 E. L.

McT. It's no use—in spite of that brutal Tottle, I can't resist the temptation of the liquor—I must have some—beg, borrow, or steal.

Dex. (*without*). Tottle, ahoy!

Tot. Muster Dexter a-hailing. Here's his dry togs! Aye, aye, sir.   [*Exit,* L. U. E.

McT. Sentinel off his post! Now's my time! (*steals up to store tent—rushes in—seizes a couple of bottles from store,* L., *and is retreating* 1 E. R, *when* Lovibond, *who has been watching him, jumps up and seizes him by the collar.*)

Lov. No, you don't, though you were ten times McTurk!

McT. Oh, mercy! mercy!

Lov. Drop those bottles, sir! I saw you take them.

McT. (*passionately*). I couldn't resist it—I feel so weak—I've such a craving for it! Oh, sir, let me go, and don't tell 'em, 'sir, don't; I shall be disgraced—cashiered. I'm a gentleman, sir—an officer.

Lov. Is this the fire-eater I was afraid of? Listen! I'm Mr. Lovibond, the gentleman you had the impudence to challenge.

McT. Oh, I beg your pardon, sir! Only let me go, and I'll make any apology!

Lov. There! I forgive you! Put back that beer. For shame of you! to try to rob a poor man of his beer! (McTurk *makes an agonized gesture of entreaty, but quails under* Lovibond's *eye, and sneaks up to the tent, replacing the bottles, and exit,* 1 E. L.) Poor, abject wretch! He deserves pity more than punishment.

Enter Miss Colepepper, 1 E. R.

Miss C. Mr. Lovibond, what is the meaning of the strange scene that has just passed in the hospital? Mrs. Sebright came in with your friend.

Lov. I know—Moleskin! Then the boots *did* fit him?

Miss C. They seized that poor lunatic—searched him—took him out of his bed to a neighboring spot—to which in the strength of his frenzy, he led the way faster than they could follow. I followed. They dug up something from the sand, and brought him back exhausted—but calmer.

Lov. (*dancing*). Huzza! huzza! huzza! Downy's done, at last!

Enter DEXTER, L. U. E., *with a small black box.*

DEX. Miss Colepepper, (*puts box in her hand*) your father's vouchers.

MISS C. Mr. Dexter, you have risked your life for them!

DEX. (*coolly*). Oh, dear! no. Only wetted a suit of clothes. I dive like an otter. Take them to your father.

MISS C. Yes; but in your name: (*crosses* L.) How often are you to be our preserver? [*Exit*, 1 E. C.

DEX. It's time to serve out the rations. (*goes up to tent* L., *and strikes gong*) Tottle!

Enter MRS. LOVIBOND, 1 E. L.

MRS. L. I can't find that dear doctor.

Enter COLEPEPPER, *and* MISS COLEPEPPER, L., *crosses to* DEXTER.

Lov. (*down on her* R. *side*). Because you would go to look for him. It's all right, doctor! The real Downy's discovered! it's your mad patient!

COLE. God bless you, sir! Mary has told me all. You have saved our good name!

DEX. Who was the fool who said "Chance ruled the world?"

Enter SMART, HARDISTY, MRS. RABBITS, LIMPET, GRIMWOOD, AYAHS— PASSENGERS, *male and female,* CHILDREN, LASCARS, SAILORS, *etc.*

DEX. Now, then, ladies first. Come forward in the order of your messes. (SIR SOLOMON *gives a strange cry without*) Hollo!

SIR SOLOMON *rushes in* 1 E. R., *wild and excited—his basket lid tumbling over his eyes—the handkerchief which bound his jaws waving in his hand—he gesticulates with vain efforts to speak articulately.*

DEX. Another *coup-de-soleil!* Get him down—put a quantity of ice on his head!

SIR S. (*speaking with difficulty*). Not—sun stroke—steamer——

DEX. What does he say? Can anybody make it out?

[*down* L. *of* COLEPEPPER

Lov. (*rushing forward*). Oh, I know the physic he wants! Open your mouth. (*produces the artificial teeth.*)

SIR SOLOMON *snatches teeth and goes up and turns his back to audience and places them in his mouth and begins to speak volubly.*

LIMP. Master's minerals at last, I do declare! Well, I'm glad he's got his teeth again, for they're not only *white* but they never ache!

SIR S. As I have recently been unable to enjoy the pleasure of social intercourse, owing to the inconvenient circumstance——

DEX. Hang it, Sir Solomon, cut it short! You can't be allowed to pay out all your arrears at once.

SIR S. Well, then, to cut it short, there is a steamer making for the reef.

ALL. Hurrah! hurrah! hurrah! (*display the wildest signs of joy. All turn to face the sea—*LOVIBOND *up a little—*DEXTER *seizes a glass and looks out—*SMART *and* HARDISTY *do the same—the crowd give way for them.*)

Enter Mrs. Sebright *and* Moleskin, R., *crosses to* Lovibond, L.

Mrs. S. What's that I hear? a steamer? (*goes up to crowd,* c.)
Mole. (*to* Lovibond) I've got him! It's Downy, sure enough.
Lov. Of course it is! Now I'll trouble you for those boots.
Mole. They're so damp I can't get 'em off. [*Exit* Moleskin, 1 E. L.
Lov. He's gone off with my boots!
Mrs. L. I'll follow him and make him give them up. (*Exit,* 1 E. L., *returns immediately with one boot*) I've only got one, dear.
Dex. Do you make her out, captain?
Smart. The man-of-war steamer "Blazer."
Mrs. S. Jack's vessel! (*jumps with joy, then half faints.*)

Sir Solomon *and* Colepepper *rush up and support her—the passengers and others are watching the steamer—*Dexter *and* Miss Colepepper *converse apart.*

Cole. Give her air, sir, can't you?
Sir S. Give her air yourself! I insist on my right of supporting this lady.
Cole. On the contrary, sir, I claim that as my exclusive privilege.
Sir S. By what title, sir?
Cole. As her intended husband.
Sir S. That, sir, is the foundation of my claim.
Cole. Pooh, sir!
Sir S. Pooh to you, sir!
Cole. She revives—ask her?
Sir S. My pretty Jane——
Cole. My dearest Jane——
Mrs. S. (*extricating herself*). Gentlemen, you mustn't——
Sir S. You accepted my diamonds—accept me!
Cole. Diamonds! (*contemptuously*) My shawl and my hand with it!
Mrs. S. Oh, Mr. Dexter! (Dexter *down* c.) I thought it was all right, and here it is as bad as ever again! Will you explain?
Dex. Not I—do your own explanations.
Mrs. S. Then, gentlemen, I'm sorry I can't have either of you!
Sir S. ⎱ You can't?
Cole. ⎰ Why?
Mrs. S. I've neither hand nor heart to give. I gave both, long ago, to Jack.
Sir S. Jack?
Cole. Who's Jack?
Miss. C. Mr. Dexter has explained all to me—this lady is married already!
Sir S. ⎱ Married!
Cole. ⎰
Sir S. But my diamond necklace, madam?
Cole. Keep my shawl as a wedding gift.
Mrs. S. Thanks, Mr. Colepepper! Sir Solomon, I'm sorry I haven't got your diamonds!
Sir S. You haven't! Who has?
Dex. I have!
Sir S. A light begins to dawn on me. (*to* Colepepper) Of course, this is Jack? (*pointing to* Dexter.)
Cole. Of course, it is! How blind I've been!
Dex. No, Mr. Colepepper, my affections are better bestowed than on Jenny Sebright—good little soul as she is—for all her feather head!

COLE. What! you are not Jack? And you don't love Mrs. Sebright? and you do love somebody else? Why, then, it can only be—(*looks at* MARY.)

DEX. It is, sir!

COLE. Take her, my boy; you've won her fairly!

DEX. And with Heaven's help, as fairly will I wear her. (*embrace.*)

SIR S. But my diamonds, sir?

DEX. (*aside*). Which you accepted from the Nawaub of Ramshackle-gur.

SIR S. How do *you* know? I mean, how dare you insinuate?

DEX. I don't insinuate; I assert!

SIR S. Only hold your tongue! I make a present of them to your wife!

DEX. My wife wears no diamonds less pure than her own bright eyes. I keep the necklace to return it to its lawful owner. I owe the poor Nawaub some compensation for the physic I gave him.

COLE. But, after all, we've never heard who Jack is!

SMART. A boat from the steamer! (*shout.*)

Enter CAPTAIN SEBRIGHT, SAILORS, *etc.*

MRS. S. Jack! (*she rushes into* JACK SEBRIGHT'S *arms.*)

ALL. Hurrah! hurrah! hurrah!

TABLEAU.

PROPERTIES.

Three dusters, for STEWARDS; cups and saucers for tea; glasses and soda water; telescope; list of dinner places; note-book; card for DEXTER; pith cap and umbrella; stick and umbrella; novel; shawl; footstool; cushion; bird-cage; shawl; brandy bottle; worn letter, for MRS. LOVIBOND; diamond necklace and case; towel, for LOVIBOND; box of pills; vial of medicine; sticking plaster; several boxes and trunks of luggage; hat-case; portmanteau; legal papers; cigar; handcuffs; card; lamps for companionway; trumpet; boatswain's whistle; barrels; cases; bottles; meat cans; flag; musket; cutlass; market basket; hamper; set of teeth; several bottles; small black box; small looking-glass.

STAGE DIRECTIONS.

R. means Right of Stage, facing the Audience; L. Left; C. Centre; R. C. Right of Centre; L. C. Left of Centre. D. F. Door in the Flat, or Scene running across the back of the Stage; C. D. F. Centre Door in the Flat; R. D. F. Right Door in the Flat; L. C. F. Left Door in the Flat; R. D. Right Door; L. D. Left Door; 1 E First Entrance; 2 E. Second Entrance; U. E. Upper Entrance; 1, 2 or 3 G. First Second or Third Groove.

R.   R. C.   C.   R. C.   L.

The reader is supposed to be upon the stage facing the audience.